# AFSAANE

a collection of short stories

## Ameya Bondre

© **Ameya Bondre 2019**

**All rights reserved**

All rights reserved by the author. No part of this publication may be reproduced, stored in a retrieval system or transmitted in any form or by any means, electronic, mechanical, photocopying, recording or otherwise, without the prior permission of the author.

Although every precaution has been taken to verify the accuracy of the information contained herein, the author and publisher assume no responsibility for any errors or omissions. No liability is assumed for damages that may result from the use of information contained within.

**Disclaimer:** In this work of fiction, the characters, places, and events are either the product of the author's imagination or they are used entirely fictitiously. Any resemblance to actual persons, living or dead, is purely coincidental.

First Published in December 2019

**ISBN: 978-93-89763-07-2**

**BLUE ROSE PUBLISHERS**
www.bluerosepublishers.com
info@bluerosepublishers.com
+91 8882 898 898

**Cover Design:**
Chinmayi Chavan

**Author Photo Credit:**
Durvesh Sawant

**Typographic Design:**
Namrata Saini

**Distributed by:** Blue Rose, Amazon, Flipkart, Shopclues

To,

the endless hours of rumination

the matchless tugs-of-war
between what's in the mind
and what's on paper

Tear off the mask.
Your face is,
    glorious.

- Rumi

# About the Author

Ameya Bondre is often crunching numbers, drafting research papers, or studying the medical side of innovative health solutions. Writing has been a reliable companion for years, but he formally began writing short stories in the winter of 2017, to finally put them in this anthology. When he is not lost in a riveting thriller movie, or regretting the absence of a dog, Ameya loves reading, banter, or day-dreaming! He is a public health graduate from Johns Hopkins University, with prior medical training at KEM Hospital in Mumbai, the city of his childhood, where he stays with his family.

# Gratitude

I am indebted to the following friends and colleagues, not to mention voracious readers, for their feedback, support and encouragement for the initial drafts of the stories: Joydeep Ghosh, Subbu Ramchandran, Surabhi Ranjan, Radhika Mujumdar, Prince Nadar, Shambhavi Singh, Pawankumar Patil, Arpit Awasthi, Anam Shaikh, Tanvee Priya, Gitanjali Pillai, Alaknanda Sengupta, Vicky Lewis, Madhumitha Chandrasekaran, Anoop Singh, Deepak Bhardwaj, Nithish Nair, Divya Udyawar, and Aniruddha Mokashi. Maybe I have missed some names, but I want to thank all my friends who read a few or all of the stories and gave honest feedback. They have an indispensable role to play in making me realize that I can publish this book.

I am grateful to the authors and editors who put in precious time and effort to provide extensive and valuable critique, comments, and edits for the stories: Himali Kothari, Vinitha Ramchandani, Varsha Naik, Vrinda Baliga, Harika Bantupalli, and Abha Iyengar.

I must thank the entire team at Blue Rose Publishers (New Delhi) for their unwavering support and hard work across all stages of book editing, preparation, production, and distribution, and I cannot thank them enough for their words of advice and wisdom at every stage.

And, I would like to thank my cover designer, Chinmayi Chavan, for the exquisite reflection of ideas best representing the stories on the cover. I am thankful for her perseverance, dedication and remarkable attention to detail.

Finally, I want to thank my family for a nurturing, flexible home, much needed in the making of this book! I don't know how I can thank them as words will always fall short.

# Preface

Writing has always been a constant companion, but it never found a roof. It's one of those things where you can take years to understand whether you have an ability. And while doing so, I stumbled upon a creative writing workshop, two years ago at St. Xavier's College in Mumbai. As hasty as I am in taking some decisions, I enrolled for it, thinking that I will use the channel to learn some techniques and structure an aimless exploration of ability. Maybe, give shape to a long, dragged, on and off relationship with a blank page of Word that I fill and erase in cycles... so much to expect from a workshop!

To quote Hemingway, "there is nothing to writing. All you do is sit down at a typewriter and bleed". But, there is a lot of humility in the relentless back and forth that the process involves. On some days it feels impossible, on others it is thrilling, and yet, on others, it seems pointless. Before you turn these pages and read the stories, I must acknowledge that the workshop, at least, proved to be a definite (re-)starting point. The periodic writing assignments became opportunities to think and draft full-length stories, the feedback sessions became reasons to edit and recast scenes, and even the lectures (such as those on 'point of view' or 'setting') became triggers to construct stories in certain ways. I surprised myself by writing more than half of these eleven stories in the last months of 2017 and dedicated the following year to edit and rework them, write a few more, and most of all, reflect on whether I could dare to compile them in a collection. And today, I pack them in this book!

Several people, places, exposures, and experiences have nourished these stories. All fiction derives from life, but that happens in strange ways. You have a heartfelt conversation and you forget it, and after weeks or months, a part of it springs out of your head, while you stare at a computer screen grappling with a different unrelated story. You realize why it stayed with you, you think harder and take a leaf out of it... and you develop and remould that leaf. You are tempted to use it or store it for later. No - this is not the only way in which life feeds fiction! Perhaps, all we need to do (easier said than done) is keep our eyes and ears open, always!

These eleven disconnected stories are about usual people in unusual situations, or unusual for their context. They dwell on feelings of love, separation, friendship, hurt, hope, acceptance, nostalgia and many more. I have often written from the first-person point of view, which I found most comfortable and direct. And, they will emote, speak, emphasize, describe and try to involve you at (hopefully) every step!

The objects you see on the cover are crucial story elements. They speak when words fall short or characters hesitate to emote. At times, they try to hold the plots or set the scenes. I have depended on them for a large part of my process, so they had to fall on the cover.

Choosing an atypical word for the title was a conscious decision. 'Afsaane' means 'tales', 'fiction' or 'romance' and

I could not find a better English word to subsume these meanings!

That's that. Now, I welcome you all to the lives of the many characters that breathe in these stories... their conversations, their hopes, and their surprises. I hope you enjoy reading them as much as I enjoyed their company.

# Contents

Distances ................................................................... 1
Dreams ..................................................................... 14
Blinkers on ............................................................... 19
Chaos ....................................................................... 35
A Regular Date ......................................................... 53
Trapped .................................................................... 68
A Healthy Home ...................................................... 84
Not in the Dark ....................................................... 104
A Frantic Call .......................................................... 127
Deaf ......................................................................... 144
Long Lost ................................................................ 165

# Distances

A bunch of European cities was trapped in the crisscrossing panels of the black showcase fixed to the living room wall. Five horizontal and four vertical panels made up the fifteen-odd shelves that hoarded memories. I had imagined arranging palaces, squares, museums, bridges, arches, and towers on these shelves. Instead, she had filled them with sandals, bicycles, ice-creams, mugs, seashells, and earrings! Each one of them wanted to jump off their space to explore our home and enter our conversations. Looking at our frequent arguments, they changed their mind. This piece of furniture on the wall is our only child. We love it. Even today, I give it the attention it craves. Why else am I reminiscing over our whimsical collection of memories? And... why does she take so long to get ready?

I gazed at the bedroom door, which remained still and shut, then returned my attention to the showcase.

The pair of miniature red heels stood at the centre of the middle shelf, the ones she had insisted on buying on a crowded street in Barcelona. They were a reminder of the time she had worn a similar pair while learning to dance the *flamenco*. The first day at *Escuela de Flamenco José de la Vega* had been a disaster. Each time she got carried away by the music and the fluttering red ruffles of her black dress, I lost track and stomped on her heels. In another instance, she tried to echo the lyrics she hardly understood, didn't pay attention, and her feet slid between mine! I clutched at her waist trying in vain to stop her fall, but mercifully, she caught hold of the shoulder of a hefty Spanish lady who was lost in her own rotations. She loved the training and adamantly wanted the heels. She claimed that the training helped her 'focus'.

"How long will you take?" I shouted. We were still young, and inexperienced in our equation, our home and our routines, and at times, my patience ran thin.

"Just five minutes. Have you taken the file?" Avni shouted back from the bedroom.

"You have asked me three times since morning." I lowered my voice. There was no reply.

There were other souvenirs from other times. A pair of tiny polka-dotted coffee mugs was a tribute to a quiet brunch at the *Antico Caffè Greco*, the oldest café in Rome. After a toxic argument, while climbing down the Spanish steps and onto *Via Condotti*, we had craved coffee.

What did we argue about? The usual but important stuff - why does the world intrude into our space, or more specifically, my parents. My mother had called me early that morning, panic-stricken, to inform that the caregiver took a sudden leave and my father threw a tantrum to avoid his pills. He screamed, which he never did earlier, and refused his breakfast. Scrambling to find a replacement at such short notice, I couldn't help peeping into my phone every few minutes and making calls, interrupting Avni's flow of conversation - she was gazing at a church and telling me what she felt, or an anecdote that I can't recollect. I wasn't telling her the reason for my distractions to avoid an argument in the middle of crowds thronging the place, and I stretched it for as long as I could, but that irritated her more. She finally got into the matter, made a few calls herself and managed to find a therapist-friend to come in and help. At the cost of getting upset, cold and distant.

At the café, we settled down at a small three-legged round beige table surrounded by maroon chairs and sky-blue walls studded with rows of framed murals. It was a noisy evening. Locals had filled the place with their rising and falling Italian accents and intense conversations. We didn't talk the whole time. We sat, gazing from the murals to the people to our golden rings and back to our coffee mugs brimming with cappuccino. We had read that the café was a 'timeless place that helped people to unwind after heavy sightseeing'. But no café could contain our relentless spirits. We had to take more calls from home. We had to stay updated. We had to pass on more instructions to my Mom and Dad. We had to follow-up. And, *we,* didn't talk the whole evening, and night. Next morning, she was chirpy, once again. Mornings made her normal. A day later, while leaving Italy, we came across two mugs in a gift-shop that reminded her of Greco. And, now they stood on our showcase.

"I am trying to find my *Aadhar* card!" she broke into my train of thought.

"Come on!" I grunted.

"It's somewhere in the folder. Don't worry, I will get it."

A pair of black and pink toy-bicycles were tied together with a cheesy red ribbon, to recollect our morning in Amsterdam. We had pedalled over the friendly streets past the steeples, the old houses with gargoyles and ornate façades, the hundred-odd florists trying to get our attention, the lush green parks, and the city's vivacious waterways. I can't deny that I cherished the bicycles. Oh, and the earring! One of her old earrings got stuck on my shirt button at the Grand Bazaar in Istanbul! We were walking like a spectacle, the right side of her head attached to the middle of my chest. People had a field day staring and giggling at us. She enjoyed walking with a slanted trunk, listening to my hammering heartbeats and couldn't stop laughing. I avoided the glares and stares, and the teasing people offering help... and tried to escape that frenzied place. And on returning to India, she showcased *this* earring! It sat next to her version of a *Gelarto Rosa*, an ice-cream in Budapest where every cone is made into the shape of a rose. She made one using colour paper, with alternating layers of brick-red and lemon-yellow petals and placed it on the showcase, claiming that the ice-cream was her 'best European memory'. She could have chosen better things from our month-long gruelling vacation. Yet, how can I forget the white pebbles she gathered straight from the clear, sky-blue waters of the *Agios Dimitrios* beach on one of the Greek islands. For a change, it was I who asked her to collect a heap of them, for the showcase, to which she said, *'Since when are you into these things!'*

"Okay let's go." She stepped out. Avni liked to startle others - then and now.

"You sure you have all your documents?"

"Please, let's go."

By the time I had locked the door, she had scurried down the stairs. I saw our name-plate for the last time. An hour-long winding ride down the hill awaited us, and at the end of it, the district court. The untimely, breezy, romantic weather gave us unwanted company. My open-top car felt unnecessary. We were not going on a honeymoon. We were going to file for a divorce, to separate for good.

We set off and within a minute, she got started, "Why do you wear faded jeans?"

"What's your problem?"

"We are going to a court, Aman, for God's sake."

"My jeans won't change the judge's decision."

"It's a formal occasion!"

I scoffed. She didn't belabour the point. That was one advantage of separating - as a wife, she would have gone on endlessly. I wanted to be quiet. I wanted to drive. I wanted to look ahead. But I couldn't.

I just had to get the words out: "After we are done, I need to rush back home. Papa needs me."

"I know that." She paused. "Why do you have to say that to me? Like that?"

"I just mentioned it," I heard my voice rising.

"Look, by now, your family and all your relatives know that I have failed to take care of your father."

"Please don't start..."

"No, seriously—"

"Do you realize his illness? Alzheimer's? And how

much we need to look after him? And, I mean, as a family – from now, it will be just me and my mother."

"And I tried that too. For two years, I tried what I could. I helped with everything. But I cannot be chained to a house."

"I don't know why his illness needs to conflict with your dreams and choices. All I asked of you was to slow down a little. I have a nine-to-five job. I have pushed my goals aside because of his health. I am going slow."

She snorted. "Yes, slow in all things, except when it comes to kissing someone."

I couldn't reply. I should have predicted that. Of course, she *had* to bring it up. And make it sound as though that one single incident had been a habit, something I did as a matter of routine!

We had fought almost daily in the last six months or so; largely because neither of us was adequately present to attend to my father. We were torn between our work, my father, my mother's inabilities to provide the level of care he needed, and our suffocating relationship. We delayed having a child. After a long fight on one of those regrettable nights, I stepped out and went to a nearby pub. I met an old friend from college, someone I once used to have a massive crush on. I took it as a happy accident but... we connected like old times, over shots of vodka. And we chatted, flirted, teased, argued and breezed from one topic to another. Time flew. I kissed her. She didn't stop me. We didn't realize how long it went. And worse, I didn't expect someone in the pub to pass on that information to my wife. Someone who was known to us. My obsession with knowing this person's identity angered her even more. *'Why does it matter who told me?'* she had screamed, *'All that matters is what you did.'*

I admitted my guilt a hundred times. This happened a month after we returned from Europe. Europe, six months back, had come as a much-needed breather but ended up being a mix of fun, fights, fuss, and frivolity. Europe, was our last-ditch effort to infuse hope, create time and find ourselves in our marriage. Did it help? Creating an eccentric showcase of memories was her way of trying to ignite any feelings left between us. Feelings, shaken by my blunder in the pub.

"You know it was not an affair. Far from it. Yet, you allowed your lawyer to quote that as one of the reasons for divorce."

"What else I could have done?"

"What else? How can you lie?!"

"Lie?" she smiled. "Please let's just stop. I am sorry, I couldn't take care of your father. I am sorry I penalized you for kissing your friend. I am sorry I decided to file for divorce and bring a lawyer into the picture. I am sorry I damaged your home by doing so. Alright? Now, please, let's not talk."

"When did you stop loving me?" I was dumb to ask that. Horrible timing.

"Please drive."

I drove fast for the next few minutes, but then reduced the speed after she clasped the edge of the window. She kept looking out, not for one moment at me. For the next half hour, we didn't speak. She preferred to close her eyes and soak in the breeze - or so it seemed. Her eyes opened when the car went over a ditch, faster than usual. Her eyes met mine and she hinted that she wanted water without uttering a word. I handed over the bottle. Her hair gleamed in the sunlight as she raised her head and drank, holding the bottle a little away from her lips. An act so familiar that a wave of nostalgia washed over me as I watched her out of the corner of my eye. But, *she* hardly looked at me. She hardly spoke. She hardly turned my way. She hardly broke the stillness. I wondered if she ever thought about me as I did about her. She had walked great distances with me but hardly crossed the distance between us. She kept it. She liked it. She hated a part of me or hated me. I failed to understand her. But the complexity... every knot we tied ourselves in, was fully understood.

I spared a few moments, every now and then, to catch a glimpse of the small things talking to us. Unnoticeable things, in the air, on the ground, and in the sky. Things that I thought could defuse our feverish thoughts.

We were approaching a winding road flanked by the mountain on one side and the tea-farms on the other. Our journey was a mix of acute turns and straight ways. Tea-plants nestled in large groups on our left. How chaotic were they? They had hundreds of leaves elbowing each other to sip that little bit of sunlight that fell on them. But they didn't sway one bit, they stood wisely. The overshadowed leaves at lower levels were content with the used light that trickled down. They didn't demand their share immediately. They waited for their turn, for long periods of time, until the upper leaves fell, or were cut off. Circumstances ruled. They adapted.

And, in between these crowded communities, stood the tall, proud and isolated teak trees. They kept a studied distance from each other. They got their space. They were privileged to shower in fresh air and sun. They didn't struggle. No one told them to be patient. They basked in glory. But they stood apart.

I turned on the music to distract myself, but Avni butted in, "Can you switch it off? I am trying to sleep."

"But you are not."

"I am trying to. The breeze isn't letting me."

"Normally, people sleep in such breeze."

"I am not normal." She closed her eyes to shut me up.

I glanced to my right. Grey and dull-black rocks were huddled together. Green shrubs separated them. Why did they grow in between the massive, monotonous and lifeless rocks? They found water. Rocks hid a lot of water beneath them; groundwater that was scarce and deep. The shrubs snatched every drop to survive. I wondered where the desperate need to live a life, came from. Weren't they afraid the rocks would crush them? They were. Fear suppressed them. They lived their whole life like repressed, invisible souls. They never spoke out. They breathed. But they formed a relationship with scarcity. And that kind of bonding took some time.

"What are you thinking about?" She startled me, again.

"So, you are not sleeping!" I firmed my grip on the steering wheel.

"Answer the question."

"I am just looking around."

"Oh… your love for nature," she mocked.

"Don't dismiss it."

The road became straighter and easier, and I speeded up, a bit in annoyance.

"So, what is it telling you right now?" she asked

"It?"

"Your *nature*."

For a moment, I sieved her words for any genuine shred of curiosity.

"That we're going too fast," I quipped, slowing down a little. "It is constantly speaking to us, but we have to slow down to hear its messages."

She shrugged. The kind of shrug that indicates agreement with a bit of indifference. Every gust of wind that lashed us seemed to be driving us more and more apart. Our reactions were polar opposites. Our thoughts were like those teak trees, standing apart, disconnected and basking in self-glory. I didn't know how many of our feelings were real, how many were unwilling... and how many were exaggerated. The only thing we had in common was this journey we were sharing, to a common destination.

She interrupted my thoughts, "When you drive down a hill like this, do you ever feel that you will fall?"

"No."

"I mean, the narrow road, the tea-farms have gone behind us... we just have the valley by our side. The fencing isn't great. No barriers here. Do you feel unsafe?"

"When I drive with you, I think only about two people."

She didn't reply.

And, for a long while, she didn't speak. She just stared at the moving gear. Then, she said:

"You don't feel like we are on the edge? Right now? You think you are going *slow*?"

"There is no one here. I can pace up a little."

"But you are able to think about two people?"

"Yes." I nodded. "It's hard to keep that in mind every second. But I do. Mostly."

"You do… because there is no one here."

"Hmm?"

"I mean… it's easier to think about us when it's just us," she said.

"Just us?"

"Yeah, like now."

"And, how often do we get such a time?" I snatched a moment to ask that.

"Europe?"

"That was a long time back!" I said, "And we weren't alone. There was always a landmark, a monument, a statue, a promenade, some history and if nothing else, the movements of a train."

"You want to be completely alone with me?" She teased, or so I thought.

"I want to be alone, here."

"Live here? On these hills?"

"Yeah. So I can touch the clouds when they descend."

"So it's the clouds, not me." She chuckled.

"Yeah, the cloud-nine feeling."

The landscape and its quietness had infected us. A little bit of peace… it crept into the car, somehow. I can't describe exactly what I felt; all I knew was that I had felt it after a long time. I felt like stopping. I felt like telling her to step out so we could take a selfie together in the meadows, for all its worth. Maybe not just that. I wanted her to pause, to absorb the panoramic valley, the prosperity, the soaring ranges of light-brown mountains whispering to the white clouds that refused to embrace them. I wanted to stop driving and hug her. I wanted to stop.

But we had reached the town. The court-house was only a mile away.

Before the judge and lawyers, we were stiff and cold again, formal and correct. We showed the documents. We answered their questions. We clarified. We thanked the advocates. We left with our files, she clutching hers, and I mine.

We stepped out and it started to drizzle. *'Such bad timing,'* I almost said that to myself. *'It should have rained during the drive!'* I was being selfish, of course.

The drizzle changed to a shower. I had no clue what she thought, but I grabbed her hand and we rushed for shelter under a bus-stop. I released her hand, but it felt stiff and hesitant. I didn't know what to make of it.

After some time, she pointed to something and said, "What's that?"

"A tea-shop."

"Really."

"Yeah!"

"It's pretty small and makeshift."

"Hmm…"

"Well, well… It has something amazing!" She squinted to catch a glimpse.

"What?"

"Look carefully!"

"Tell me."

"You have to see it."

"Come on…"

"Look! It's something you love," she said.

I peered through the falling rain and caught sight of the brown cups without handles. They had *kulhad chai*.

"Awesome!" I stopped short of jumping in delight.

"Remember you complained every fourth day in Europe!"

"Yeah, I wonder where else in the world they have it."

"Should we have it?" she asked me.

I nodded. We had no umbrellas. And, we were not holding hands anymore. We walked along, with a bit of distance separating us. We got drenched. No, we didn't look at each other. We wanted to have *chai.* And, while I can't be sure of her, but I wanted some time. A little more time, for us… we couldn't have asked for more.

# Dreams

I walked for six continuous hours. I, walked six hours without a break, in anger, weaving in and out of crowds on long, noisy streets, in a tough, taunting city. I was incapable of competing. Walking made me contain myself. Another failed day at music, but today made me ponder– Why I can't take it? Why am I losing my drive, here?

It was at 11 pm. I halted at a deserted bus-stop. After waiting for a few minutes, I briskly got into a running, random BEST bus. The next moment, I heard a song. No — I heard the most haunting voice in ages. The bus was empty, so her voice floated, undisturbed, into my ears.

The viciously crooked *Raag* challenged her, note by note, but she held it firmly. There she leaned at the window, just before the driver's seat, soaking in the breeze that freed her to sing, or so I thought. The bus picked up speed. When her voice began to grow on my head, a khaki-clad man blocked my view.

I paid the fare and walked closer towards her. Rows of empty seats stared at me, almost warning me to hold it right there — don't make any sound that would break her rhythm! Inching closer, I saw that a *bandish* in *Yaman* played on her phone. I realized that it was *her* recording. Thank God she didn't use earphones, else I wouldn't have found her.

I took the seat behind her, gently settling in. The noise in my head refused to dim, after a hard day, even though the tension in my hands and legs lowered a bit. Her voice had just begun to soothe, but could it ever heal?

She was humming it, at times, seeming lost in what those words meant... Then, after what seemed like ages, she turned her face from the window to look to the other side, giving me a clearer view of those tired but eager eyes.

I straightened, breathed in a little and asked her, "Is this *your* voice?"

Startled, she turned back. "What? How did you...?"

Those were deep, black eyes that had a glow; but I interrupted. "I... I'm sorry, I'm trained in music - I know it's not the original."

"But, my voice...?"

"I guessed. Please don't worry..." The last thing I wanted was hostility. She turned back. I was in no mood to stop asking. "Are you trained in music?"

"Yes. And I don't think we know each other."

"Sure, but I can't be quiet... when I hear a voice being nothing, but true."

She looked down, at her phone, a bit shyly.

Ten minutes and we said nothing. In the next few minutes, I somehow opened up:

"I am living here since four years. I sing, but have to assist music directors for a living. I only perform in small, local shows. I feel strange contentment within, which I don't like. I can't stand it... at times, I get angry. But I learn from the big names - who don't want to give me a chance! But one shouldn't complain... right?" Her back was straight, her face tilted, a bit, to my voice. She said nothing.

I asked her, "What brings you here, at this time, with your recording?"

She turned back, and there was eye-contact. She said, "I was imagining myself singing it. Yes... to a huge, intently hearing audience, in a concert. You are a singer; you would know about imagining concerts! But *they* won't."

I got intrusive. "Who won't?" She bit her lip. I persisted, "Who stops you?"

"No one. They reason it out of me. Why – you would give me my big break?!" I saw the first smile...

She added, "And, what keeps you going?"

"I don't know. I think I can only do music, or be around music. Nothing else." The song on her phone had stopped.

Putting a tissue back in her bag, she said, "I always have to take care of my mother. She has a long-standing illness. I am lucky to have a terrific husband who understands this. I have a brother who lives abroad. My father needs help, to help my mother. I get free by 5, but, I do spend time, like this, once or twice in a week. My family knows – I stay back at the office... then take the bus... late..."

I poked my nose. "Why not tell them that you want to audition?"

"You think I have not?" She paused. "You won't get it... it's different, we are conservative. Anyway, it's tough when you have to attend to both an ailing parent and your husband — you cannot pursue other things."

"Music is, another thing...?"

"Sometimes, the only thing that makes me happy," she said.

I closed my eyes and thought about her... her being brave, taking every effort to make her mother get back to her feet; finishing her work early, to give more time to music – to remain sane. She has never auditioned. Then, her parents found her a suitable boy. And of course, she is thankful for a good husband, with whom she shares her angst to sing. He understands, but he is hesitant. He explains to her — the need to stick to reality, the futility of dreams and the tangible expenses — every time they bring it up, and she eventually agrees. She *has* to agree.

She broke my train of imagination, "I've got to go..."

"You know - I know this director—"

"Please don't. I don't want to make the hundredth attempt of convincing my husband and family."

She rose from her seat. My heart raced along with the bus, heading to its destined stop. She would slip away.

"Listen, three new singers are meeting him. But this song he's planning is peculiar and needs a fitting voice. I know. I assist him daily." For a while, she stood still, listening. Then she went ahead. I almost stopped her.

"Look—" I said loudly, "Look, I am no way saying that this would work, but why don't you just come there — just... just bring *this* recording to his office? We can meet at the cafe ahead on this road, next Monday, during your lunchtime. Can we?"

"I cannot!" she yelled. "I have to discuss with *them* each time, and it's the same thing..." She went near the door.

"You know what?" I yelled back, "Don't tell anyone, and come..."

I had walked in anger, because of my wants – knowing what I had and could not show the world. And there, she stood. I said – "Yes. Looking at myself, I cannot give hope to someone else. But, then I heard you, I heard *that* voice."

I saw her in the dark, at the door. Yet, I could not see those eyes. The driver braked, disrupting the silence. She got down and I saw her walking behind, and fading. Some people were boarding the bus at its rear door.

The bus started. I thought I heard a scream from outside – "One o'clock!"

# Blinkers on

Froth clung to the oval mouth of the purple coffee stirrer as she took it out of the cup. Placed on a barren brown table-top, the bubbles, breathless and delicate, held on to each other. Not one wanted to venture alone into unknown territory. Paper napkins lay around, crumpled and abandoned. Empty cups looked back at us.

Nisha took the last few sips while caressing the cradle. The cradle sat on the chair to her left. The chair had been pushed back to make space. The cradle was a little bulky with a sky blue arch and squatted legs curving back to join by a horizontal orange panel. Screws fixed all its joints. It was an uncomplicated piece.

But, never so simple for her. She scanned the misty window on her right. She hunted for any clues. It was pouring outside. She was transfixed. Not a word had been spoken since we had settled in. No eye-contact. Fifteen long minutes. The waitress revisited our table and asked pointedly if we wanted anything more. Nisha shook her head with a blank face and turned back to the window.

I didn't feel like eating or drinking. There was so much to digest already. How many more questions had to be answered? I didn't peep into the cradle but envied the child it held, his motionless sleep, his chest rising and falling in a perfect rhythm. Did the rain gods have any concept of timing? I wanted to step out and drive. To take Nisha home was urgent. The clutter in our bedroom would dissolve her empty stares.

A sudden burst of laughter from a bunch of college kids sitting at the next table stirred him a little. He fidgeted, made a few groans. She looked into the cradle, swayed it a little. He didn't wake up.

The kids stopped chattering. They had taken shelter in this café, thanks to the sudden downpour, to chat for a while. As we had, minutes after we had stepped out of the Centre, the place I wanted to be most further away from.

"I think we should go home." I said.

"No wait, it's raining." She stroked the sky blue arch.

"Please, let's move out," I said.

"Look outside! He will wake up in the car."

"That's alright. I am there," I said.

"How? You will be driving."

"Do you want to drive then?"

She didn't answer.

"Say something."

"Aniket, we have just got him. Do you realize that?"

"No. Because *you* are quiet. And when you don't talk, I can't think clearly."

"Well, it's you who thinks through decisions, don't you?"

"Taking you along. Yeah?"

"And with very little time?" she asked.

"That's the system. We can't help it."

"I am ashamed. I don't know why. I shouldn't be. I should be loving."

"You are."

She didn't speak for some time and rolled her fingers along the arch, as if feeling it all over again. "You know, some women after they deliver, feel low. In fact, many of them."

"And?"

"This—", she stole a second to glance at his sleeping body, "this is not even that. This is something we have invited. I am scared."

"Don't say that. It's our family."

She went mute. It looked like the foggy window gave her company.

She had a point. We didn't get much time or say in the matter. They told us that the process had been simplified, the rules had been changed. Parents uploaded documents into a centralized system. After matching their preferences, the system allowed the parents to see only one child in each round, and a choice had to be made within 48 hours. They had abolished the practice of 'pick and choose'. Children are not commodities, they said. Parents must accept whoever they get. Just like normal biological parents do. It had all sounded fine. If we rejected the child they offered us, they would show us another child based on our preferences, after 90 days. Oh yes, they did not exclude preferences like age, state, and gender. Perhaps they could afford not to, as long as their registry had some

2000 children. They gave us three rounds. After the third round, we would have been pushed down a waiting list of 15000-odd parents if we hadn't made up our minds. And so, we accepted. We wanted to fill the void.

"Nisha."

"What?" She looked at me.

"I love you. And I love Akshay. Stop thinking. For some time."

"You are calm, aren't you?"

I sighed. "I think so. I love him."

"I know. You've said it ever since you saw his profile."

"Yes."

"Which I cannot ever fully understand. Is it instinctive? I mean, it should be," she chuckled. "But, doesn't it take… time, for you?"

"Are you happy?" I asked her for the millionth time.

"Yeah," she responded with the millionth meek vigorous nod of her face, as though to emphasize. "But aren't you worried?"

"I have stopped worrying."

"Don't lie to me."

"What do you want me to do?"

"It's easy for you. I am the one who will be looking after him all day," she said.

"I will too, when I come home from work."

"You will be exhausted."

"I will be eager. To be with you both."

"When he sleeps."

"I won't be so late. I promise."

She gave a purse-lipped smile.

"When you resume work, at a later point, you will feel better," I said.

"It's not about work! I don't intend to resume. I'm in no frame of mind to work."

"Okay." I paused for a bit. "We have a new maid. You chose her. You are content with her. She will help you."

"I wish your mother would." She closed her eyes and inhaled. "I – I am sorry."

"Give her time. This is a big shift for her."

"And for me."

"Of course."

"You know what you don't get? It's not the specifics. The nappies, the tantrums, the playing, the feeding, the lack of sleep. It's not about that."

"What is it then?"

"Something more. I want to feel the same as your mother felt, or mine, when they had us. I want to experience the same things. When I look at him, I feel I care. But not strongly enough. I love him. But, it, does not overpower me."

"Give it time."

"And to deal with this all alone? I am the caretaker. I am the one at home. With... with a stranger. With no support from your parents. And, hardly any from mine."

Her voice cracked a bit, as if bearing the weight of her words. Before it could fragment any further, I withheld a reply. A reply from my end was needless. There was no way I was going to elaborate on her point of being unsupported and dissect the topic and ultimately let her cry. Both of our parents had become reticent. As if they had given up. Let the kids decide *whoever* they want to bring home. I rewound to the question of whether we had little time to take this decision - perhaps the reason for her turmoil.

"I know this has been fast. This will feel abrupt. We got three chances and we decided during the third. It feels outrageous. I know."

"Stop reminding me of that, please."

"Biological parents just get one chance, Nisha. That's what I'm trying to say."

"Are you seriously comparing? You just said it. They are biological. That takes care of everything. Including their fears."

"No. People fail. They make mistakes all the time. Ask parents of one-year-olds."

"It's different! They have several months to process their emotions about the new arrival. They *get* those several months. It's internal, for them. I don't believe the way you are trying to reason this out."

"Okay, I will stop."

"Besides, the family helps them. Overwhelmingly."

"Agreed."

The pouring reduced to a drizzle. What a relief! Now I could take them home. I insisted. She relented. Anyway, she was sick of my attempts to console. I let it be. But to take her home was needed. At least, she could be in a different place - and ponder, think, analyse and build castles about our situation, at least, in a different room.

A fifteen-minute drive, but I chauffeured them gently. Akshay didn't wake up. I wished he would sleep all day. Or at least for the next few hours.

We reached home, a home waiting for us with a hundred things to be done. We were just back, with our child, fighting the odds we could.

..................................

It was yesterday, in the evening. I had to visit my mother, who stayed about twenty minutes away. A lot had to be said there. A lot had to be heard there, which was imposing and unwilling. Nisha knew. She was prepping Akshay's room, moving around, tidying things to ensure it was spick and span. She didn't care that the room would gather some dust by tomorrow morning, hours before Akshay's arrival, because she would clean it again to her satisfaction. I went near her, almost to stop her, and turned her around.

"What?" she asked, her eyes bore into mine, almost closing their lids. I kissed her. She got still for a moment, then let her eyes open. She mumbled, "I am okay, Aniket." She kept her head low.

"You sure?" I tried to look into those eyes.

"Yes, you can leave me alone. In fact, it's better you do."

"Why?" I rested my forehead on hers. She sighed.

"I want your conversation with them to go well," she said.

"That's a tall order!" I chuckled.

"It's worth trying. Go… and come back soon."

"Should we call the maid now?"

"No, in the evening. I don't want anyone here. Just me and his room. He... will come tomorrow."

"Yeah," I looked at the empty cradle. "Okay. Bye. Call me if you need anything."

"No, I won't. I don't want to interrupt your conversation with them."

Dad opened the door. He smiled and hugged me. The gesture was devoid of any celebratory feeling. But I sensed vigour, at least. He was seventy, a year older than my mother. Any ounce of vigour was useful. I could extract something positive, something naïve, something silly and hopeful out of it! Celebrations could wait.

I had barely taken a seat at the dining table when Mom pounced: "Who is he?"

"Please listen."

"No, tell me, *who* is he?"

"I don't know."

"Do we know his community, his birthplace?"

"No."

"Do we know the kind of parents he had? Their education? Their values?"

"No."

"Didn't you ask about his origins?"

"They don't reveal such things. It's not allowed."

"Why?"

"It's not legal."

"Oh, is it?" she smirked.

"It works both ways. We are the legal parents now. His real parents can't... just take him away from us."

"You are foster parents. Till the court ruling. Don't forget that."

"Okay. So, we will become his legal parents in a year's time. Happy?"

"When he grows up, he will have legal rights to meet his real parents," she said.

"Let him meet them. Besides, not all children want to do that, just for your information!"

"What if he wants to? What will happen then?"

"I don't know. By asking me again and again, for the tenth time, you think you will get a better answer?"

"Aren't you scared about it?"

"Of course, since you keep reminding me."

"Do you want to share your child with anyone else, even emotionally?"

"No. Can I just assume, for now, that he won't want to meet them?"

She shook her head. "I don't feel he is ours. Yes, we saw the pictures. You told us everything. But now that he's home, I feel strange. I don't understand what was the harm in trying IVF again."

"Please think about us. She had an ectopic pregnancy. Twice. We went through multiple IVFs. It only made us hopeless."

"I told you about surrogacy."

"And you know we wouldn't do that. It's a transaction."

"Transaction?"

"Yes. We were both utterly uncomfortable with that idea."

"How is adoption not a transaction? You paid money."

"Akshay was abandoned. Left to the mercy of fate and strangers. For a Centre to care for him. For reasons that he doesn't know and perhaps will never know. But he has *us* now. Now, do you understand why we are more comfortable?"

"He is someone else's. Just doesn't feel ours. He is from another family. Another culture. Another household. Another pregnancy. Another mental make-up."

"So is Nisha. But you claim that she is your daughter—"

"Aniket. No," Dad interrupted. Mom folded her hands and furrowed her brow. I didn't feel like looking at either of them.

"He could turn out to be a different person, regardless of your nurturing," she said.

"What about us? Nisha? Have we turned out to be as expected, or different?"

"Don't argue with your mother, Aniket. And don't divert the topic," Dad snapped.

"I am not - how have I turned out to be, tell me? Am I a mature adult? I think I have harassed you enough. Especially all these years after marriage. No grandchildren! Is that kind of stress, something you expected from me when I was born?"

Mom took a deep breath and replied, "She had ectopic. You both had failed IVFs. You didn't want surrogacy. You both liked this child. But you convinced her. You registered for this process. One thing led to the other. She took it as it came. And now, he's home! I am sure she is in panic mode—"

"So, what are you getting at?"

"Do you see what you have done? It was not a complete decision."

"We have waited for five years. I am thirty-five. She is thirty-three. Akshay is seven months old. I am happy that if not from the beginning, we at least have him now. We feel complete. At least I do."

"And Nisha doesn't?"

"I know what's grappling her. She is anxious, scared, confused and even ashamed. But she doesn't want to change anything of this."

"The incompatibility between you both and him - as a separate individual, have you thought of that?"

"That's our responsibility. My responsibility. He is my son—"

"Who is seven months old. Time will fly. He will go to pre-school. Children are smart! And not kind. What if someone tells him casually, what if it gets leaked to him, his identity, the concept of not being born to you? In a very inappropriate manner?"

"There are ways for parents to tell children, early. We will do that."

"How?"

"I don't know. I haven't thought of that yet."

"How many times have you said so far, that *you don't know*!" she said.

"Keep counting."

"Do what you want."

"Well, at least you are right about one thing. Nisha is in panic mode. I must leave."

My Dad intervened. "She just wanted to be honest with you. She had a lot to say and ask you." He was in spokesperson mode. I smiled at him and walked towards the door. My mom sat where she was, staring into space, her brow still furrowed, her breathing heavy, her arms folded tight across her. She didn't budge one bit. I left.

On the way home, I got stuck on a congested road. I peered at the children selling pirated novels at the traffic signal. I thought about their homes, if they had any, their people, their environment. I noted their restlessness, their curious smiles, their shabby clothes and their apparent ease with the total lack of security of their circumstances. Anyone could rob them of their money, give them drugs, or traffic them to another world. Walking and talking bodies, living on the edge. Looking at them, I felt a perverse sense of relief at my own situation. I didn't know where that came from, that feeling. It was sick. Why should I feel relief? They were children! Why was I comparing them with my son? Wasn't there anything else I could take out of their situation? Something hopeful? Positive? The signal turned green.

..................................

That... was yesterday. Could it be a bygone? Who knows.

We reached home and finished the hundred things we had to do – settling Akshay, who still had his eyes wrapped tight, and settling ourselves. I wanted to bury my head into a pillow. Or take a hot shower. Or have coffee. Or lock myself up. But there he was, the new member of our family, asleep and dreamy. The air-conditioner helped him. Nisha was shuttling nervously between the kitchen and the bedroom.

I took a chair and pulled one more in front of it. I patted it. "Come, sit…"

"Don't tell me what happened last evening."

I kept mum.

"We avoided that topic, whatever your parents said yesterday—"

"I know."

"And we will avoid it now."

"We will have to face it, Nisha."

"Aniket?"

"Okay… Okay, I won't". I grabbed her elbow.

"Anyone…", she smiled, "anyone can look at your face and make out what happened. What must have happened." She caressed my head like I were a pup. I had always adored that gesture, to bits.

"Stop… don't think about that." I pulled her down on the chair. I held her hands and opened her palms.

"How are you?" she asked.

I couldn't speak. Just nestled my cheek on her palms.

"Sometimes you confuse me more than a seven-month-old child can," she blurted.

"He is a fine guy. Isn't he?"

"What happened to you?"

"Nothing. I am tired."

"And?"

"I don't understand why we can't take things one step at a time."

"Hmm…"

"You can?" I asked.

"Yeah. I will have to. I will." She said.

"I will walk with you." I didn't let my cheek leave her palms.

She hugged me and fondled my hair. I didn't let go. I wanted her to shield me from all the noise, all the questions. She mothered me. I let her.

"I am scared too," I whispered.

"I know."

"Lot of thoughts crowding my head."

"No, there's nothing. Look at me." She kissed me.

"Tell me something…" It was my turn to question. "You still thinking as you were in the café?"

"Oops." She got up all of a sudden.

"What?"

"He is making sounds," she said. The groans grew louder.

"Yeah, he is waking up."

We went to the cradle parked next to the window. The drizzling had disappeared, but we hadn't noticed. A strange unexpected sunshine seeped into the room.

Akshay was awake. Deep black eyes greeted us. I pulled down the blinds a little more to block the piercing sunlight. He recognized us. We had ensured that we had made the most of our first visit and the time we spent at the Centre that morning. He reached out with a small hand to touch my nose pointing at him. He barely stretched his hand. He smiled. He shifted his view and gazed at Nisha. He stared at her for a while and blinked. It looked like he pointed to her earring. He babbled a few *aaaam*'s and *ummm*'s. Nisha cooed at him. I could have gone on... looking at the two of them forever. His index finger was a reliable guide. She brought herself closer and he tapped Nisha on her chin, and tried to reach her cheek. He sensed something large and sky blue above his head. He looked up and tried to reach for the arch of his cradle. She lifted him a little. His hand, now outstretched, touched the arch. He laughed. He returned the favour by smiling at her. He groaned a little more. He fidgeted some more. Perhaps he was eager to free himself. Like us. He yawned a few times to shed any remnants of sleep. I lifted him out of the cradle and started talking, showing him his room, and opening the cabinet gently to reveal all his little toys—the trains, the planes, the ships, the cars, the robots and what not! He squealed in delight and tried to grab the objects. I sat on the floor, with him on my lap, and we explored the cabinet.

The phone rang. Nisha went to answer it. I watched her as I guided Akshay.

"Hello. *Namaste,* Mummyji." I made to get up, but Nisha waved me down. She hinted me to stop.

"Yes." She took a breath. "Yes. We all came some time back." Nisha stared at me while talking to my mother. "We left the Centre but it started raining. So, we stopped for some time and... we got late." I had no idea what the voice on the other side was saying. Nisha turned quieter by the minute. She listened with great attention. She became motionless, her eyes flung far at the open window. They almost stopped blinking. She looked at me, her eyes trying to convey a hundred words, nodding all the while. I searched her eyes for hints, even as she gestured to me to stay where I was. If only I could figure what she felt. She seemed to bear it, and take it all in. All that she heard. All that she was told. And whatever she could believe or disbelieve. Suddenly, her eyes welled up. I got flustered. But then she suppressed a smile and bit her lip. She nodded her head in agreement. She let out a suppressed laughter.

And, she said, "Tonight, tomorrow, whenever. We are waiting. Please do. You and Dad. We *all* want to meet you. Come as soon as possible!"

# Chaos

A pair of empty eyes stared at the drenched window. A raindrop fell on the pane, slipped along, and stopped for a moment. He saw dozen-odd clones. They joined hands to change shape and make their way through colonies of thousands. Crooked rows that formed and died. Like the raindrop, he stared at. It made a slender line on the glass that glided for a while ... and then broke down. Little pieces with nothing left to speak.

Few more drops fell, carefree and least worried about their fate. They sprinted, halted and settled in. Stuck on the glass. Hurried. And hushed. They made no sound. Until the stroke of a windscreen wiper bulldozed them. The driver turned it on, making a dark, grey, drop-less rainbow that broke his train of thought. Crushed all the colonies that formed in his head and pushed his clones away.

In no time, a stormy rain flooded the window, which shone fleetingly with flashes that bounced on and off from streetlights. Inside, the numb seats of a locked cab lay rested. Amit's bag huddled in a corner, pressed against the other door. His head remained still and staring. He could not talk to the massacred colonies of raindrops. Deluded to think that they wanted him. Hardly. The thousands of them made their own groups. They were meant to pull him in. Entice him. Throw him down memory lane. But they ran their show. There were no gatekeepers to let him enter. He had few turns to take, to speak to them. Till he was blocked. Outcasted. There was no one else. No voices to be heard. Only a body unmoving, and a mind brooding.

"Am I a fool?"

"Totally," Nikhil said with a blank face. He knew everything about Amit's state, or the only one who knew. So, he didn't want to leave him, all by himself.

Nikhil was the kind who would say a lot, but wouldn't express what he felt. He found it tough to comfort someone, even his close friend – or just say something that could soothe. He would bend down his head a little and stare into space. But he never found the words, the precise words. He wasn't cold, but, his ways were rather straight — just be with the person, stay there, give him company, respond to his quietness by yours. But sit there, just stick on.

Yet, Amit didn't want him to come along, all the way. A part of his mind didn't want to be alone, bearing *it* all. Another part acted stronger.

"Do you want to head back?" Nikhil stopped the elevator.

"No."

"Why are you forcing yourself?"

"I am not."

"Of course you are. You don't have to go there. No one would miss you there."

"I was called."

"Out of courtesy, Amit. Can't you see?"

"And I want to be there. It will give me closure."

"Far from it! You are just trying to be a good person. You don't want one bit of this."

"Please. Let it be." Amit made a straight face. He had to make him agree.

The elevator raced down.

"At least make yourself tidy," Nikhil said after they stepped out. "Go, freshen up. I will wait in the parking lot."

Amit rushed to the restroom on the ground floor. He hated the clear wide mirror. It revealed his face. Exposed him and his intent. All the colours that he could see. All that he hid. He hated it. The drooping shoulders. The slight furrow on his brow, which stayed, unless he forced it to disappear. A smile that did not erupt, not even a suppressed one. He hated the mirror. But looking away was no better. His black leather shoes were dusty at a few corners. Devoid of the blackness and stripped off their shine. He tried tidying up. The white shirt tucked out a little from the side. The grey trousers were disinterested. The quiet shadowy pits below his eyes screamed for attention. He splashed some water on his dry face. That was that. Neatened his hair a little, so they didn't look rude. The tie was tucked away inside his bag. Hidden. Crumpled. It had no place elsewhere.

"Is that what you call tidying up?" Nikhil mocked, no sooner he saw him sitting alongside the front seat.

"Listen, I will order a cab. You go home." Amit unbuckled the seat belt and barged out of the car. He pulled out his phone and tapped the screen, harder and faster to search his cab.

"Right. So this is what you do? Get mad at me."

"Because you are not helping, you see?"

"I am not? And what are you trying to do anyway?"

"I am trying to face it. This is what I need to do. One last time."

Nikhil stepped out and banged the door. He didn't look straight at Amit. He gazed along the roof of the car. He bent his head down to muster all the energy he could, folded his hands and took heavy steps to come to the other side. He hugged Amit much to the latter's detachment. He withdrew a bit, hesitated and let it go, but blurted out.

"Look, you promise me one thing."

"No, I won't."

"You will do this, okay? You will go there, yes. You will stay calm, meet whoever you want, stay for a while — only for a while, yeah? And leave."

"I can't promise that."

"Look… I know, the matter—"

"Yes, you do."

"But maybe I don't know *you* as much. But for my sake."

"I don't know how long I will stay there. How can I promise?"

"All you wanted was to be there. Right?"

"So?"

"So, that's what you are getting to do."

"And?"

"And that's what you will do."

Amit didn't answer.

"Amit?"

He didn't reply.

"You heard me, right?"

He kept shut.

"Please?"

"Okay."

"You still want to go alone?"

"Don't come with me. Don't wait there. Let me do this."

"No—"

"It might rain. Then you will get stuck in traffic. And you have to go very far."

"Please cut this crap—"

"Listen," Amit sighed, to gather his thoughts. "Well, okay... think of it this way... it will be more difficult for me, with you, because I would see you getting affected as well. Will that be useful?"


That's how Amit got in the cab at around 7 pm. A half-open window meant no calm. The road was familiar. A recurrent street that took him to work daily. A familiar sight in a bustling city. Boring, busy and bantering at the same time, but the one that lit up in the evenings. The track was long and winding with traffic, noises, horns and busy movements of people jostling each other, elbowing, siding by, and wading through, to reach their homes, stations or bus stops. The street darkened by the minute. The wind lashed at his face, the cars screeched into his ears, and the passing groups of college boys and girls giggled in his head. He looked sideways and saw the restaurants and cafes glittering in evening glory. Their loud flashy lights seeped into his eyes.

A little boy looked about three-feet tall, he had brownish streaked hair and a dusted blank face. He wore a tattered red T-shirt and jaded black shorts and rolled a tyre with a stick. He pushed his way through groups of people who rushed against him at times, near the edge of an uneven footpath. They blocked him and let the tyre slip away. Each time it fell, he lifted it and continued to roll on. The tyre found its gaps and spaces to keep running. He let its pace pull him along, mindless and carefree and lost in the motion of the lifeless, abandoned object.

Engrossed in the journey and not where he was headed, he went along. A minute later, Amit lost him in the crowd.

And, where was *he* headed? For whose sake? Even an aimless rolling tyre, falling and standing under someone's command, was a better state to be in. His mind wavered. His thoughts laboured. His eyes searched, searched helplessly as they sifted through the tyres of cars, the pebbles, the trash, and the tar, and the shoes and footsteps of others.

That's when it began to drizzle. Shower. And pour out of nowhere. And he thanked the rain gods, so he could shut himself in. Close the windows and filter the noise a little. Stare at the windows in the dead quietness of his locked cab. To see the glass getting drenched and the colonies of raindrops forming in. Making a display. Whispering in their little private groups.

Could he throw his thoughts away? Memories. Words that hurt. Could he talk to these people? To the groups of friends laughing at the corners of this street. Couples parked at motorcycles, immersed in conversation and sharing cuddles that they wanted to hide. Old couples walking slowly with nothing to say, but tonnes of unspoken affection. A child clasping his mother's hand and taking tiny steps with a yellow school bag on his back. And, the people chatting inside locked cars. But not his cab. With no sound and no chattering that followed… unlike, when Aditi was around.

"So, is this the last time?" he asked her.

"Yes."

"Look at me and tell me that it's the last time."

"Amit?" She fiddled with the straw sloping on the rim of the glass.

"No, look at me?"

"Does it matter?"

"Yes, look at me… please."

She did. But their eyes hardly met. It was a long, dragging conversation that had screamed its way to a dead-end. The decision was taken. He had to abide by it.

"Being friends is not healthy. Not for me and definitely not for you." This, is what she said.

"Because I fight? I go back to our memories? Is that what you mean?"

Amit had tried different ways to hold the conversation.

"No, it's your face… the way you speak," she said.

"You provoke me. We meet, we talk, it goes well for some time—"

"Oh, does it, really? Does it go well?" she heckled.

"Yes it does," he paused. "And let me finish — then, it's as if you must — must pass that one remark, must say that one word, or something that breaks me, something that cuts me off—"

"And, then what do *you* do? Don't you go on a rampage? You go back to your grudges, our old fights. You pick up an incident, and you make me remember it? All the way? Why? Because I say something that cuts you off?"

"Aditi, we are hurt. We don't like the fact that we fight. We have never been like that—"

"Whatever we may have been earlier, this cannot continue the way it's going."

"You know that's not what we came here for. We came to arrive at something. Some form of resolution—"

"No—"

"At least something concrete."

"And *that* does not mean a relationship. Perhaps not even a friendship."

"Please listen to me…" Amit got fidgety in his chair.

"No. Do you even realize that people who don't move on, who cannot get over their broken relationships, can, still, have, a reasonable conversation? At least when they meet after a long time, which we are unable to."

"Who are these reasonable people if I may know?"

"We don't make each other happy," Aditi raised her voice and lowered it quickly, watchful of the people around. "Please understand that! We don't — even in the most normal conversational ways. We make each other angry. And when you don't want to accept that and hold on to something that doesn't exist, I get more upset because..." She sighed.

"Because?"

"Because I don't want to reach a point where I start pitying you."

Aditi said that and broke eye contact. That's all she could do, stretch the extent of her part, her problem, and her emotion.

"Go on, continue," he said.

"With what?"

"With the pitying."

"What the hell do you mean?"

"To hell with dignity. Aditi, if you want to be someone who feels bad for me and just that, then be that person. I will take it. It's better than fighting. The loud back and forth. The tone... all this we end up becoming. At least, you would *be* with me, that way. A friend can pity, right? Can look at her friend with empathy? You can do that too. And be with me. I don't care if it's called pity. So long as it keeps you with me."

"So that we keep meeting?"

"Just tell me what makes you happy and I will bring it to the table."

"I love..." Aditi stopped to pull in her thoughts. "...the flight of pigeons. Do you remember?"

"Jama Masjid, yes."

"Right. Think about them. They swing up and down. Keep a rhythm. A distance from each other. But they are together. I love the water that drips from the edge of a grill — you know, after it stops raining, those drops that wait… and gently slip off? They make me smile. Smile. And, I want that. When I stare at those, they make me feel wanted. Do you get that, Amit? When I see you, I just want to look away…"

She paused again, to think. As if the choice of words mattered any more. Amit got colder and clueless. She carried on:

"… I want to look away, but I cannot do that, right? I have to talk to you. I don't want to be rude. But when I try to talk, things happen between us. Ugly things. You say the nastiest things. I react. You break me. I hurt you. And it goes on, and on."

"No, it does not," Amit denied in vain. "We do calm down."

"No, we don't. In fact, it keeps going on inside our heads. Just shows what we think and what we have, is hopeless. And after it ends, I want to laugh at myself for trying. Trying to talk to you."

She got up, pulled out her bag from the hook of the chair and left the next moment. He never saw her again, nor the café where they met, with an aim to resolve, but ended up arguing and creating the little tugs-of-war that never broke. Unlike their relationship.

And, a year had passed since. She was precise. She wanted it. She executed it. He saw that when she left. He didn't see it coming, that day. Not this way.

The cab jerked at the next signal causing some relief to Amit and his frenzied train of memories. He checked the map and saw '12 minutes'. He opened the camera of his phone and rotated the view. He looked at the face he saw, adjusted his hair. But the eyes failed him. They would communicate exactly what he did not want them to. They spoke when they were supposed to be quiet and docile. They didn't know how to put on a show, like he thought he could. They didn't know that the smile on his face came through them, and it was bound to appear fake. They didn't think about him, nor his smile. They showed their true self.

They say, love yourself. Take care of your body. Think good. Forgive. Absorb. Love yourself and let it speak through your face. He had become the subject of these words, which began to deafen him over time. Even someone like Nikhil, who knew, began to use these clichés beyond a point. He could not control his silences, which in fact, were stronger. He had to say something, so he fell for these feeble overused words of advice.

Why blame Nikhil? Even a parent did not see through the core. She could see something odd, her questions always unanswered. Her patience tested to the limits. *My child is an adult now, I should not bug him again and again* — is perhaps what she thought. But that troubling ignorance... why did he want to be left alone. She couldn't do much about it.

His phone beeped. A chat window popped up to demand attention. He opened it, and questions pounced on him, one after the other.

Mom: Did you reach?

Amit: Almost

Mom: Did you leave straight from work?

Amit: Yes

Mom: Did you freshen up?

Amit: Please

Mom: Okay...

Mom: I was surprised that you agreed.

Amit: I am not.

Mom: Okay. But it's been a long time. You could have avoided.

Amit: What do you mean?

Mom: I mean, when did you last socialize, in this way? More than a year back.

Amit: So?

Mom: I don't know much. You don't tell me... anything.

Amit: There is nothing to it.

Mom: You don't tell me anything. Even when it hits you. Changes you.

Amit: Listen

Mom: Makes you into someone I don't know.

Amit: What??

Mom: Why don't you tell me?

Amit: Haven't I, in the last week? When you restarted this topic?

Mom: There is more to it. I am not dumb. Why don't you tell me?

Amit: Tell you what?

Mom: I can see it, even without looking at you. I can

see it right here, in this chat.

Amit: She is a friend. A friend, who is out of touch. She got back. I am invited this evening, and I am doing the needful. That's what I have been telling and repeating in the last one week, haven't I?

Mom: And that's what I don't understand.

Amit: Let's stop this now? I have reached, I need to pay the driver.

Mom: Okay.

He left the chat window.


He stepped out of the cab, and after a while, a message jumped high, to spiritedly climb onto the screen with a loud beep. Something was badly left to be said.

Mom: I forgot to tell you

Amit: What?

Mom: In the morning you were looking good. The rich white shirt. It suited you. You looked good, yeah?

Amit stared at that message for a few seconds and typed 'okay' as a reflex. The fingers lost any thought that was left unsaid, from the long day, but his eyes welled up. They had taken in way too much. He felt heavy in his throat. Because, his mom could only see the good in him, even though she knew something was odd. Just so she could make him feel better. She just saw the things that made him a good person, but he didn't want affection or praise, after a flurry of memories were left behind in the cab — and in the last one year and more. There was no strength left, for praise. He blinked hard, to kill any tears that could have formed, and set off. A grand spectacle greeted him. A ceremony.

A gate of sunflowers was carved into a broad arch. Broad enough to let a dozen-odd people walk in on the maroon carpet that welcomed them. Multiple rows of flowers were stitched together. The yellow sunflowers sat next to the saffrons, the reds were juxtaposed with the whites, and pairs and groups of bright pink tulips separated the rows at uneven intervals. The yellows looked radiant and inviting, with their broad dense-brown crowded centres, and the happy bright petals that stood almost straight — or shook a little with the passing wind, foolishly thinking that they stood in an open unshackled field under the warm welcoming sunrays. The red ones were a dark brooding presence, with petals that didn't make a noise about them. The emerald green bulbs on the surrounding coconut trees splashed their lights onto the arched gate and the sunflowers could only beam in glory. The women weren't left far behind. Their white, beige, green and yellow sarees sparkled in the artificial light with their golden borders, their studded necklaces and their beaded edges, their clinking bangles, their dangling earrings, and their smiles — their warm, amiable smiles. The place was lit up. Prepped. Made to draw you in, to entice an outsider and a member alike.

He was neither. But he was approached by an elderly figure, just a few steps inside the gate.

"Amit?"

"Yes?"

"I am Aditi's teacher. How come you forgot?"

"Oh yeah, sorry Mr. Das. I was just finding my way in. Didn't notice you right away." He chuckled. Amit had uttered a lame reply. But normal, something normal maybe, given the long day. "So, does she still learn the guitar?"

"Very much. If she would have stopped after a year, I wouldn't have been attending today." Mr. Das giggled. "But you just vanished, didn't you?" He quickly brought the focus back on Amit.

"Did I?"

"Yes. You were her audience! She used to tell me, with such excitement, each time she learned something new and played it for you, and came to my class with your reviews!"

"Oh yeah... that."

"You had become like a sounding board, for her, and for my teaching." Mr. Das gently took Amit by the side of the carpet, so he didn't block the people who gave him the cold stares.

"Sir, if I may, I will just meet Aditi and get going." Amit didn't want any memories Mr. Das had to offer.

"Get going, why? Stay here, we will chat."

"No... I will have to. May I?"

"Oh sure, okay." Mr. Das smiled. "Please meet them. Before you have to stand in a queue."


And no sooner had Amit found himself inside, inching closer to the stage, he was greeted by curtains. Alternating pink and white standing curtains made a blinding backdrop. Carnations, tulips, roses — rich, deep pink roses, made a horizontal panel on the top, and a few were stuck on the flowy delicate curtains, such that they had begun to dangle under the cello-tapes. Some had fallen on the stage. Some had been crushed by kids running behind the couch — a small white couch with golden pillows and golden edges and legs, at the centre of the stage, stationed the bride and the groom. They had grabbed a moment for themselves, with glasses of orange juice. Visitors on one side had climbed down the stairs. Those waiting on the other side took a pause. Small groups of families were crowding downstairs. Amit was standing right at the centre of the alley between the rows of seats, but at a good distance from Aditi. All she had to do was to look straight, and she could have caught him, for that little, broken, short-lived moment. But the groom engaged her. He whispered something in her ear. She giggled. He went on with it. She giggled more and told him to stop. And he agreed. The little eye contacts. The warm smiles, the flirts, and the sweet-nothings. They were lost in their madness, uncaring for the people that scrutinized them from their seats. And all that Amit could do, was to watch them for a while. And leave.

He took a book out of his bag, wrapped by a gold gift-wrap paper with a red ribbon on top, and a handwritten note on a yellow paper tucked underneath the ribbon. He turned around a little, to see Aditi again, clenched the book tightly and hid it behind folded hands, seeing her content, happy and enchanted by the workings of the place, and her husband. He left them and while walking out, saw Mr. Das seated and busy looking into his phone. He held a firm grasp over the book to cover the ribbon, and stood before him, till he was noticed.

"Hey, Amit, you met them?"

"Yes." Amit gently pulled out the note from the ribbon and hid it in his trouser pocket.

"What's that you are hiding?"

"Nothing. Would you do me a favour?"

"Sure."

"Can you give this gift to Aditi? I met them but forgot to hand it over. It just stayed in my bag," he said.

"Okay, I will. What is it? Oh sorry! You mind me asking?" Mr. Das was visibly curious.

"Not at all. It's a book. I made it. Each page." Amit sat down next to him and said: "It has a collection. Notes and chords. All the lessons, the songs, the rhythms you taught her. She had once forgotten her music book at my place. So, I re-made them in — well, in this sort of stylized way, you can say. Each page has a lesson of yours. And followed by an explanation — for that song, or chord, or notation. Just something relevant about that piece. Its usage, or its origins, or its history, or analogies in other forms of music, any variations, or songs that have used it. You know, the challenge… the beauty… the workings. I had to do a fair bit of fact-finding for this. But I tried as much as I could. Just think of it like your recreated music book, for her."

Mr. Das looked at the wrapped book for a while and didn't speak a word, then held the book firmly.

"Amit, this — this is really special. Before I say what I think — can you please go up and hand it over to her. Yourself."

"What she has, at this time, is way more special." Amit smiled, nodded, and got up to leave. After he had walked several steps, Mr. Das called him:

"You will still not give that note, which was under the ribbon?"

"No." Amit smiled at him and waved.

The note was not meant to be a part of the gift. Something he knew, but he deliberately put it in. Something he should not have. It was meant to engage him further, in her and her life — a life that had nothing in it for him. Like a hundred broken drops sliding on a cab's window. Like a child's toy-tyre lost in the crowds. Like Nikhil's failed attempts to convince him. Like his mother's ignorance of his matter. The note had to lose its relevance. It said.

*When did the sky fade? Where did the stars drop? Where have your songs gone? Did we miss them, or they drifted apart? Did we find them — or did we stop? I have packed them in, for you. Maybe, you will throw it, at last. But you can peep in, a little. For the sake of what we lost.*

*— Amit*


He didn't know what else he could do. But he could smile... smile at someone, while leaving the place he wanted to avoid. A day had gone by, in thinking about this evening. That ended briefly, but with some shape. He felt something concrete. Far from a comfort or anything like it. No, not a completion. Far from a closure. But he felt like a start. A little shred of peace. An untangling that he felt in his nerves. Maybe, it had just begun.

# A Regular Date

We met on a shimmering, moonlit night. The still waters of a blue lake mirrored the moon, the swirling bits of white clouds, a few scattered stars and the twin summits of a snow-capped mountain.

We found ourselves in the middle of a circular boat floating lazily on this lake. We carved small circular tracks on the water, circles that kept shifting their centres. Our boat was like a giant porcelain dish with an ornate blue carpet at its centre, and raised edges crowned with multiple rows of lilies, roses, and carnations sewn together. The creators had taken great pains to make it special. Hundreds of white daisies, magnolias, and tulips were strewn on the floor. The sound of a shy, soft trumpet, the source of which we couldn't find, rose and fell in perfect rhythm. It was our night! A night on which we could forget the *Hows*, the *Whats*, and the *Whys,* and simply soak in the fragrance, the music, the lights, the caressing motion of our boat, and each other's presence.

We sat on slender teak chairs across an oval plywood table placed at the centre of the boat. We held in our hands, Bordeaux glasses half-filled with a young *Cabernet Sauvignon*, a rich ruby liquid with a tinge of magenta on its edge. A pink candle at the centre of the table, armed with a jet black wick, dazzled in its own light. A million drops of white wax took birth and crawled out of its mouth, forming slender glaciers down its sides. They trickled down... seemed to fear every moment and hesitate every bit along their brief course before crashing on the plywood. And the clouds! Cheerful, mischievous clouds came sneakily upon us in gossipy huddles, till we caught them right next to our boat, peeping at our glances and smiles and stares and blushes, and eavesdropping on our conversation. Guilt-stricken, they sprinted away.

This night, like several nights before it, refused to repress its many gifts.

And yet... she appeared thoughtful, a bit removed. Yes, she smiled, but wasn't in it. Did she know? Did she wonder at my intent? I could only imagine the questions in her mind: What would this meeting lead to? Why had I made the sudden call? What did I wish to tell her? She looked me in the eye, then blinked and looked away. There was no dearth of things to look at, in *this* place. Her gaze flitted from this to that, to finally land on the candle burning between us.

"So, is this why you left me?" I asked, turning my head to my left and right, taking in the beauty I was thrown into.

"What do you think?"

"Look at this place. Who wouldn't want to live here?"

"Didn't know I would end up here," she smiled.

"So, you guys are never told about your new homes?"

She nodded in agreement.

"Is it always so bright?" I asked.

"Kind of. But tonight, they decked it up for you."

I scoffed at that line, then changed the topic. "What are your days like?"

"Sunny. Busy."

"Busy? In this place? I don't believe you!"

"Pranav, I do have work to do."

"Really? Like what? Sunbathing?"

I knew she would strike back. "Excuse me, I write," she said. "See that maple tree? I sit there. Stare at the lake. Kill time. Till thoughts crowd my mind. And then I put some on paper. During the day, the lake takes on different colours. Flickering, gleaming yellow. A tinge of gold."

"That inspires you?"

"Maybe. Then I try to hide from the winds. They creep in though, they are naughty. They try to blow me down memory lane. They don't let me write."

"Oh, they don't let you miss me."

"Not one bit."

"I miss you Ruhi."

"Even now?"

"You don't believe me?"

"It's been five years," she said.

"So?"

"Are you sure?" A small smile played on her lips and vanished.

"Does time matter?" I asked.

"They say it heals."

"It hardens. You think that's healing?"

"Maybe. But, not for babies," she said.

"Go away!"

She giggled and sipped some more wine.

"Do you really think about me, when the winds leave you alone?" I asked.

"Early morning? Hmmm... it's quieter then."

"I didn't ask how it is."

"Empty."

"Answer my question!"

"Why do you always need validation?" she asked. She knew well how to dodge me.

"I don't know. I don't have you around anymore. It's been far too long. Maybe I have gone mad."

"No No... you just like drama," she said. "So... what's happening in your world these days, Mr. Social Media Guru?"

"Don't ask."

"Tell"

"No!"

"I want to know about your world too."

"Okay." I sighed. "People hiding behind machines. Push-button commentary. Trolls. Bullying. Abuses. Name-calling. Slut-shaming. Body-shaming. Fair skin fascination. Misogyny. Filth. Sleaziness. Sting operations. The stalking, spying and snooping. And the debates!

Gibbering. Glib talking. Taking pot-shots. It's endless. And – and this need to display, just about anything! To show... well, a class, as if there's any such thing as that... People venting out. Frustrations. Outrage. Anger – anger bottled up for way too long. Only to spill over on posts and comments. And, the screechy moral *Gyan*. Dress codes. Food codes. Culture codes. Language codes. Manners. Love thy country. Love thy God. Love thy clan. Love thy family. And attack the other."

"Hatred?"

"Yeah."

"So, say it's hatred. Why complicate it?", she gently shrugged her shoulders.

"I am an analyst. My job is to read this shit day in and day out and try to make sense of it."

"And what's your conclusion?"

"That I should stalk you, and stay here!"

"The first, you already do. The second, you shouldn't." She narrowed her eyes a bit as if to gauge what would I say to that.

"Okay, but I am frightened. I am losing my friends. I am isolating myself. I am overworking. I am reading twisted stories about twisted people. I am so happy we didn't have a child. I would have freaked him out, today. No, I am not suicidal. Not yet. But without you, I don't feel like living there."

"I know your friends well. At least some of them. They really want you and they... they are there." She arched forward and said, "Don't be stubborn."

"I don't want compassion. I am sick of it. I want them to be normal. And somehow they never are, are they? They can never be." I took a deep breath and hid my face in my hands.

"Pranav... I left it all. I can't fully know how you feel. I am selfish."

"No, you are soothing. A million times more than this lovely place of yours."

She coughed, or faked it.

"Okay, just a *little* more than this place." I smiled and avoided her glance.

"Dog!" she said. "Is this your build-up?" I could see her eyes getting curious.

"My build-up?"

"Yeah, to lead me on to something?"

"What?"

"That's what you do. Don't you?" There she went on, quizzing me.

"What?"

"The *how-much-I-miss-you* story will soon turn into the *I-want-to-tell-you-something* story." She got the words she wanted.

"There's no story. Nothing important." I sipped a little bit of the wine and tried to hide behind the Bordeaux glass. It couldn't cover my eyes.

"Are you making new friends?" She went for the kill.

"Friends?"

"Yeah? Heard of 'friends'?"

"I just said I am losing them!"

"New ones. New friends?"

"Not really."

"*A* new friend?"

"Come on."

"Just because I live here in this dizzyingly exotic place doesn't mean I have no contact with... as you say, your world."

"You wish!"

"Stop it and tell me!"

"It's not what you are thinking."

"So, who is she?"

There she guessed it. I asked her, "Did you spy? Or, just look down? Ask your sources? Take time off your writing and your life to check on me?"

"No. Else I would have tweaked my questions. Trust me, I have no idea," she said.

"Well—". It was time to reveal. I pictured *her* for a moment looking at the calm waters of the lake and turned to Ruhi. "I - I met her on a plane. Four months back."

"This is so *filmy*—"

"No, wait. It wasn't. Her name is Tanvi. In our first meeting, she lied to me that she was married."

"How did that come up? No no, wait. Tell me from the beginning." She leaned forward, resting her right cheek on her right palm, a teasing smile on her lips.

"Okay. So... she... well..." I grappled with my pauses. "She had this... alluring hairstyle."

"Uh-huh?" she prodded.

"A mix of wavy and straight. Tinges of brown, but mostly black. A beige *kameez* and a light-orange *dupatta*.

Sharp features. A smile that gently made its way through her cheeks and seeped into her eyes, making her whole face glow. An earnest voice, but ...you know... the one that... tries hard. A bit nervous. Flustered. Intense black eyes. Searching. Searching for... I wondered what. She held her shoulder bag close, almost hugging it—"

"Were you smitten?" Ruhi interrupted, her interest aroused.

"I was floored."

"Yeah, you sound like you were. Tell me more, this is exciting," she rested her glass of wine on her chin.

"You are sick. We are on a date!" I said.

"We date every week. This is different! Come on, tell me more."

"How can you be excited?"

"Come on, this is spicy! And the place where we are now?" She chuckled. "This lake. These clouds. This world. There are no judgments here."

"Clearly."

"Tell me!"

"So, I offered her my aisle seat and took the middle one."

"Why?"

"I don't know. She asked me. I agreed."

"You tactical you."

"Yeah," I smirked. "And, so... maybe that's why we went on to talk. Our purpose of travel. Work. Bosses. Clients. Deadlines. Routines. Lives. Cities. So, Tanvi also lives in Mumbai."

"And that's when you spoke of marital statuses?" she asked.

"Ha Ha. No. She blurted it out – '*My husband hates me taking flights after 10 pm.*'"

"Huh? A flight's not exactly a rickshaw or an Uber! Assuming he comes to pick her up!"

"Yeah, it sounded like that. Whatever. Anyway, it turned out later that she had been lying all along. I mean, technically," I said.

"You guys met again on another flight?"

"No, no! We…" I smiled. "We exchanged numbers."

"Numbers?" Ruhi raised her voice. "What? You? Of all people? You took her number?"

"One second! Tanvi is into PR. Not unrelated to my field. And we spoke a lot about work. So, I had to."

"Dog! You actually—"

"Shh! And, about two weeks later, I pinged her. We chatted for a while. First, just the regular stuff, this and that. Then, I brought up this upcoming conference in Mumbai for PR professionals, which she wasn't aware of. Strange. I… well, I almost asked her out… I mean, I asked her if she would attend the conference. I told her I was attending. And I texted two smileys. You know that blushing smiley? I know, I know, it's ridiculous. Don't laugh."

Ruhi put her glass down and laughed. I wanted to throw a big ball of tissue at her. But I had made her laugh. That was the reason I visited her. It made my date. She went on to probe: "Okay, then?"

"So, we met again, at the conference," I said. "And again, the next day. For coffee. And sometimes wine, like this. Dates that were not even remotely close to ours. But yeah…" I took a gulp of wine.

"And that's when she told you more about herself. And corrected the facts."

"Yeah. She had separated from her husband. I felt a surge of relief. But I also felt, uh… strange. Confused. Twisted, all over again. I tried calling you. You were untraceable. My thoughts were too scattered to listen to your voice in my head. I wanted firm, clear advice. Sleep evaded me, or came in pieces. Daydreams stopped. Images blurred. All I could think of was how you could be found."

"Here I am." She picked up her glass again, sipping the wine to process her thoughts.

"What should I do? Tell me."

Ruhi didn't answer immediately. She stared into the glistening blue waters of the lake with the wine clinging onto the edge of her tilted glass that rested on her lips. She didn't take the next sip and blurted out:

"Pranav, do you really miss me?"

"Every day. Can I please sound hopeless, horrible and hideous, and tell you how?"

"Go ahead. I am used to it."

"Early morning. Hot water. Coffee. Just the right teaspoon of sugar. The fine line between waiting and turning over a *dosa*. The tantalizing *tandooris* you make. I wonder, who else in the world can make those? Tolerating the maid's tantrums to retain her. Your knowledge. Your memory. When to change the pillow covers, when to replace the bedsheets, when to clean the furniture, when to call pest control, when to call the gardener for the plants, when to dump the old utensils, when to ransack the wardrobe to give away the old clothes. I am tired, Ruhi. I can't eat without you. I order food, sometimes deliberately, to make myself feel that you are not at home and that's how I should manage. I can't watch a single movie without you. I don't listen to music before I sleep. Every bloody song reminds me of you! Yes, all those crazy songs, the tackiest, cheapest, silliest, brain-dead horse-shitty shrieking lacerating songs! From the Biebers to our item numbers. The moment they played, you used to shake and sway on the bed like a hypnotized toddler. You and your street tastes!"

"You. Are. So. So. Bad."

"You put me in a cage. Sheltered me. Tamed me. Formed my habits. And now I don't know if there is any real freedom outside, even if I were to fly."

Ruhi blushed. She had a peculiar way of being embarrassed. She would restrain a smile and look at my wrist, or my ring, or my sleeves, or my shirt collar - just about any place that would keep her gaze away from my eyes.

"But will this PR chic fill any of these major gaps in your life?" She giggled.

"Don't elevate yourself so high. She's not bad!"

"Really?"

"Yeah."

"Will she make you refrain from smoking and drinking?"

"I have reduced. In fact, it's zero. I mean, smoking, since the last two months."

"I know. *That* I have definitely been keeping a watch on."

"It wasn't easy. But it's the one thing I don't do now, which makes me proud," I said.

"And will you listen to her, if she asks you to... for this, and everything else?"

"I am not sure. I will try. But I won't smoke or drink. I know I have no sense of balance there."

"Beyond that. Will it be the same?" Ruhi tried to read something between the lines, or what she saw.

"As in?"

"Listening to Tanvi and listening to me, will it be the same?"

"Never. How can it be?"

"Are you trying to find me in her?"

"Silly. I can't. In fact, I will live with both of you. One, on the clouds, and the other..." I grinned. "I'll use every ounce of my selfishness."

"Does she know that?"

"She doesn't know about *this* place. She doesn't know our regular dates - our lake, our boat, our flowers, our moon, our starry nights. But she knows I am full of you."

"Why would she agree then?"

"She is lonely. Like me. And we gel."

"Minimum needs. Bare essentials?"

"Yeah."

"It doesn't sound like you need advice now." She said that with blank eyes.

"Ruhi, I won't take a step without you."

"Do you want to live with her? Live-in? Or, you want

to be just a friend? Friend for life? Marry? Or, just travel with her?"

"I don't know. These are formats. But I won't take a step without you along."

"Pranav, just ask me what you want to."

I kept mum for a while. Tried to choose my words. She waited.

"Can I... be with her?"

Her face changed. As if she had gambled and lost. She had got the much-needed information out of me, the stories and all the spice she wanted, but it had turned pungent. She paled. The colour vanished from her cheeks. Her eyes stopped twinkling. The moonlight dimmed. The gossipy clouds withered, bit by bit. Her eyes wavered, went on a searching spree until they stumbled in their tracks, between my eyes, my lips, and my clenched fist. She guided her lips over the edge of the glass for a while. But the pretention looked inadequate. She put the glass down on the table, held it for a second, then let it go and rested her palm on the table. She felt chilly and retrieved the sweater slung on the backrest of her chair.

Pulling it on, she said, "Will you still call me?"

"Yes."

"Will you continue to come here?"

"Yes."

"Will you bore me by talking about her?"

"Yes."

"I may get drifted away from you."

"I won't let that happen."

"I hope so," she said.

"Please take me with you." I urged.

"No."

She looked at me with the glint missing in her eyes. "Pranav, it's time for you to move on. With her."

I glared at her. "I can't. And you know I can't."

I don't know how it came gushing out, the pent-up grief of five years: "Why did you *die*? Why leave me alone? Neither did you take me with you, in this glittering world of yours, nor will you leave me alone in mine?"

She held my hand for a moment, half-broken, and said: "I will leave you now. Not leave you alone, but leave you because you are no longer alone." She smiled and slowly let off my hand. "So long... until our next date."

……………………………

A baby cried at the table behind me, and I jolted awake. Shit! How had the waiters not noticed? I checked the time. An hour had passed! Tanvi hadn't reached yet. But my phone buzzed on vibrator mode, growling against the surface of the table.

I answered: "Sorry. I… uh… I dozed off. I know. This is crazy. Really sorry!"

Well, she was almost there.

"Yeah come upstairs. It's the last table on your left."

In a few minutes, she was there. Brisk. Eager. Curiosity didn't kill some cats. She turned her head to her right and to her left and fidgeted in her seat to find a place to hang her walnut-brown sling-bag. She could have just dropped it on the floor. She settled into her chair and glanced at me fleetingly before fiddling with her phone.

Why the uneasiness? It was only a decision. We could discuss, then take it or leave it. There would be no judgments. She knew it.

"Listen." She joined her hands and made a firm fist. "I know we can talk about this later. I know the dinner can come first. But, let's get it done and get it off our minds. Yeah?"

"Okay… I am ready."

# Trapped

I watched with growing concern as Divya sorted the medicines and Vishal cleared his throat nervously to give the little speech he had been preparing in his mind over the past several days.

I know, because I stay in his mind too - I have been breeding there, alternately multiplying and shrinking with time, for the past two years. I met him at his house party, when his friends tried to talk him into having me. Friends who came from similar homes - rich, reputed and wary of their statuses. They ensured that certain things happened behind closed doors to preserve parental expectations. Vishal resisted as much as he could, but after he Googled the immediate effects, the likely reactions and risks, he went ahead. And since then, he didn't stop me – or for the most part, he didn't quit. Except that, today, with Divya around, sitting next to him on his bed, and in this place filled with people in white coats, he is a bit careful.

"I've been meaning to tell you something," he said.

"Tell me what?"

"I think I am ready to move out from here."

Divya closed her eyes for a moment, then reached out and held his hand. "Look, Vishal—"

"No, listen to me. It's not that I'm tired. And it's not a random thought. It's not my overconfidence either."

"Then?"

"It's been five months here. I just feel prepared now..."

She looked at him keenly as if tracing his thoughts.

"Yes... more than I have any time before," he added.

"But *you* don't get to decide that."

"I can explain it to them."

"They won't make an exception."

"I will be better served at home, with you. I mean, if you could stay at my home. Then, they will get it."

"We still have two months, here. Why can't we just—"

"Divya, listen—"

"It's not *me*. I'm not blocking your wish! But who will listen to you here?"

"I can explain everything to the therapist. I have done my homework on this. Okay? But I want you to hear it first. Just hear me out and tell me how it sounds, yeah?"

She gazed at him, taking in his fixed, determined gaze, still brow, and a tense, motionless body.

"Okay." She glanced at the plastic box of medicines on the adjacent stool, then squeezed his hand. It was a typical high stool with typical steel-grey legs and a spotless white covering cloth, something I hated but wasn't afraid of. This place threatened me and my kin, but a lot of us had already embedded in his head.

"I will hear you," Divya said, "and then we will talk to them." She got up, releasing her hand. "But first, take these," she said, opening the box and unpacking the pills.

He watched her carefully sort the blister packs of pills, pop out one from each strip, and place it on a steel dish. She was slow. Thoughtful. She double-checked before she lifted the dish - this was only her second week... she had joined him much later in the course of his therapy.

"Divya..."

"Yeah?"

"Hmm..."

"Tell me?"

"Nothing."

"What is it?" She turned to him.

"Thanks for being there..."

She didn't smile at that. She studied Vishal, maybe trying to spot the flicker of hope in his eyes that only she could find.

But I heard that line of gratitude and went numb. It always comes when you least expect it - that crashing moment when you know you will lose a friend and there is no going back.

*I* was Vishal's friend, the selfless one. Or so I had thought. Aren't those people selfless who exist and function only to give pleasure?

But he loved Divya. They had met a year ago, but somehow quickly thickened into friends, who understood each other, and eventually fell in love. She had no clue about *me*... the only thing he kept hidden from her. She trusted him. And he broke her trust on that fateful day... So, she left him. But, something made her come back. I don't know what. Maybe she thought about it, the whole matter, all over again. Maybe she thought more about Vishal, the person she knew, than about me. Maybe she thought that if she loved him in the true sense, then she could try to help him. Maybe not commit, but at least help. I don't know what she thought. I didn't live in her mind. Or maybe, his favourite aunt spoke to her, tried to explain her. But, two weeks ago, when she came to this room, having the typical high stool with the typical steel-grey legs covered with the spotless white cloth and people in white coats, she had said – *'I am here to try Vishal. And if you lie and don't give yourself a chance, I will stop trying.'*

I had thought back then, on that fateful day... that Divya would not forgive him. Far from it, I had expected her to break it off and leave his room that very instant. Okay, they had known each other for a year. So what if it was intense, warm and sturdy! So what if they fought like teens and made up like adults in quick succession! So what if they said, often, that they didn't want to lose what they had, even if it was still... fresh, naïve and new.

Anyway, who am I?

I ... I am born to wreak havoc in minds! Inside the brain, I like to tear away the walls of cells that think and try to stop me. But, I soothe them, slowly, and set them free. It requires some work to break their fragile egos, but as soon as they begin to sway and shake a leg, forgetting their stature in the larger scheme of things, I just let them be. Soon, I transform into a relentless DJ steering a crowd of lunatic dancers. Over a period of time, I befriend their community. They need me as much as I need them to survive. Outside the body of my man, I am just an insipid particle, but inside, a raging bull.

My man - on the morning of that fateful day - had locked himself up in the bathroom. After he got done with our daily ritual, where he would unpack me and take it all in, he set off. Our ritual, behind the locked door of his bathroom, was the only time I got to know his most impulsive, eager and agile needs. I don't think his favourite aunt or Divya ever saw that raw, real side of him. Anyway, he set off to attend an important meeting.

"Why have you come in a *kurta*?!" Divya stopped sipping the fresh orange juice that she loved to have at nine every morning at this sea-side café, with an old-fashioned creaky brown door and breezy pane-less windows where they often met for breakfast.

"Because I love you. No, I love this day more than you!" Vishal briskly pulled the chair closer to her.

"A *kurta,* at this time! What did your Mom say?"

"Oh, they are too busy decorating... prepping the flowers, curtains, tables... Anyway, that's later... did you order?"

"No, I was waiting for you."

"You shouldn't have."

"Finally, it's getting official," she beamed like a sunflower, or so it appeared to me.

Vishal held her hands, turned them and went on to search something on her palm.

"You have seen my lines yesterday! What's with you and lines!" she said.

"Shh... so you are going to get married, huh? Hmm... in

a month's time," he played along.

She giggled.

"And... you are anxious! But... also curious." He looked closer at the lines. "Oh, you love him! The guy is swashbuckling, sensitive... oh, and frigging smart—"

"Is he really?"

"And his parents are going to announce something, soon, that will let two people share one life... one long, beautiful, chatty life —"

"You forgot one thing."

"Aah! I see it here. Travel - a life with a lot of travel, yes!" he said.

"We wish!"

"Oh wait... that announcement is today. Today? Isn't it?"

She nodded, stifling a burst of laughter. Vishal kept gazing at the giggling girl and her gleaming earrings. Finally, she managed to stop.

"Why do you get so unusually excited when we meet here, even before you order the coffee?" she asked him.

"I really don't know."

"Is it something about this place?"

"Umm, no".

"Or something about this time in the morning?"

"No."

"Then?"

"I just feel it from within."

"What do you feel?"

"A strange energy."

"How? While staring at my earrings?"

"Can I play with them?"

"No. First tell me, why this high energy?"

"Do you love me?"

"No!"

"Will you love me?"

"I don't know."

"Will you marry me?"

"Hmm"

"Will you?"

"Yes." She said it softly, letting a smile stay on for some time. Something he loved.

"Why are you making me wait for a month, then?" he asked.

"Oh, come on!"

He smiled and took the menu card to aimlessly turn its pages.

"Why do your eyes look watery?" she asked.

"Mine?" He wiped them off. "Were they? I don't know." He cleared his throat and shifted a bit as if to calm himself and resettle in his seat.

"Yeah, a little... but you do have a runny nose. What happened?"

"Ah. Nothing. It's just a cold." He looked down to check his shoes or something under the table, trying to avoid an answer.

"There's a slight heaviness in your eyes, but then... I

can't see it clearly," she said.

He swivelled up and smiled at her. "Oh leave it."

"Did you secretly have ice-cream before you drove down here?" she asked.

"No, nothing without you."

"And what was that grand entrance all about?" she probed. "Slamming the door open, scaring the waiter, and charging towards me like that!"

"I feel like a leopard."

"Yeah, right!"

"You got scared?" Vishal sniffed hard and set his hair a bit.

"You wish!" Divya peeped into his phone buzzing on the table. "See, your favourite aunt is calling."

Vishal told all his secrets to his aunt. He told about me too. When parents burden you with expectations and family prestige is the only real currency, you move out to other listening ears and patient heads. She was the one. Also, she counselled him. She was a practising therapist, which helped. And, Vishal always felt reassured after meeting her. Divya didn't threaten me as much as his aunt did. She helped him get out of me… for about two months… when I lived in a pack, tucked deep inside his cupboard. He didn't touch me. I didn't see him or hear his voice. Why did he boycott me? As if he knew I was hidden but deserved to be. His aunt also tried to keep me away, physically. Once, she threw me out of the cupboard, once from his car and on another occasion, even from the pocket of his sling bag. She won, on these few occasions, when she managed to dump me somewhere… and Vishal meekly listened to her. The last she heard was that Vishal had abandoned me, or so he had told her during their last session, a little more than a year ago. Till the winds changed, Divya came in the picture, their equation got serious... and his aunt, with his parents, got a bit distracted by their relationship and the marriage plans.

Anyway, I hated this café with the pane-less windows, and these coffee dates. The chitter-chatter felt like a deliberate effort of two people to remain happy. As if warm, sunny, breezy, sea-side breakfast mornings were more intoxicating than... *my* effortless natural abilities. And as if the tensions of the impending marriage were masked by the veneer of their laughter. Divya was having anxiety pangs practically every night before she slept, and Vishal had to assure her constantly that her life wouldn't change one bit when she shifts to his home. *'This is sudden. But it won't feel sudden. Trust me, we all are there for you'.* He kept telling her the same thing, locked up in his bedroom, slouched on his sofa. During these elaborate, reassuring phone conversations, he kept me away, as far from him as possible. That's what I was sometimes - a funny little being that was ready to be used and forgotten. I could not ask questions or complain. So... when she finally calmed down, he closed these chats, hung up the phone and got down to business: his routine business, which to my mind, was his real source of happiness. Or, our *ritual*, as I called it. Though one thing I must admit that he truly wanted her. He needed her, more than she needed him.

When Vishal left the café and reached home an hour later, the place was decked up and ready for the upcoming announcement. The beige sofa took centre-stage in the living room, shining under the yellow lights, studded with olive-green and brick-red cushions. The chandelier's hundred-odd tiny white bulbs had not been lit yet, but it towered over the place hanging right above a vase of fresh, radiant sunflowers placed on a circular centre-table. The walls were embellished with some old Ravi Varma murals that Vishal's mother had painstakingly unpacked from their storage upstairs and readied for the occasion. And the food! The sideboards were stacked with appetizers to kick-start the union between two families: from the likes of croissants and cheese cubes, garlic bread and carrot cake to home-made *samosas* and *gulab jamuns.*

Vishal was greeted by a barrage of questions: "Why are you wearing this *kurta* now?" "It will get creased!" "Where were you?" "Stop bothering Divya!" "I am sure, she was confused about what to wear today, wasn't she?" "What did she say?" "Did she look tired?" "Have her parents already left?" "Where are you going now?" "Vishal, listen to us!"

"Call me when they are here," he said, cutting off the questions. "I need to sleep for a while." He ran up the stairs and disappeared into his room.

The entire family, in high spirits for the mid-morning meeting, had effectively delegated the tasks. Vishal's aunt was busy making his favourite pudding. His mother was oscillating between the living room and the kitchen, trying to find a sense of calm even as she pointed out the slightest lapses to the bustling servants. The atmosphere was busy, jovial, hurried and filled with a spirit of display. In the kitchen, Vishal's mother was touched at the sight of his aunt working so hard. "*Bass Didi.* You have worked enough. Take some rest now. And please get Vishal down, if he doesn't come in the next ten minutes. They should be here any moment."

But Vishal had taken me all the way inside his bedroom, and locked us in the bathroom. Latching one of those doors seemed enough to him.

Getting down to our ritual, Vishal sat on a stool and pulled out a packet of painkillers from a deep corner of a wooden cabinet drawer. He opened the packet to reveal another thin, transparent, plastic sachet. Finally, I got a full view of the million-odd particles of *my* family. Till now, I could see, smell, and hear through Vishal's senses - see his watery eyes, hear his sniffing nose, live through his bursts of stray excited words, and stick onto his sudden high energies. But now, I could see more particles, like me, waiting to be sucked in and give me company in his mind. Quick and adept as usual, he laid out four parallel rows of white powder on the black marble surface, next to the wash-basin. He reached for his wallet, pulled out a hundred rupee note and made a thin roll of paper. He brought the conical end of the rolled paper closer to the heaped edge of the particles. The white particles shone in sharp contrast to the black marble, as they climbed over one another in a rat-race to ascend the note. Through his nose, he forced a deep breath in, and further in, to suck them in. And there it was... at last... the explosive sound I had been waiting to hear. Something I lived for! While he snorted, I heard the happy cries – my kin had entered his nostrils and in no time they were absorbed into the vessels of his brain. Merged with his blood, they orchestrated the remaining events. Vishal was breathing deeply, his heartbeats gathered momentum and he felt an insurmountable sense of relief. He loved every moment of freedom he captured through each snort. He kept smiling to himself and would have allowed himself to laugh and scream, had he been alone in this big house, with just me for company. Nowhere could I see an unstable person, someone who needed help, someone who could break down at any time, or someone who did not realize the depths he had fallen into. All that was bookish nonsense. He knew what he wanted. And, he was happy.

Until he heard vigorous knocking on the other door, the door to his bedroom that was unlatched.

"Open the door!"

"Aunty... uh... w-wait...", he fumbled.

"They are already here. You have to come down."

"Wait, I am just getting ready."

"Getting ready? For so long? What's going on?" She sounded to me as if she had seen it all coming, in her head. Maybe it was his urgency, the way he had climbed the stairs. Maybe she saw something.

"Please, please, just give me five minutes. I will be down. You go ahead."

He hurriedly wiped the marble and covered up the traces of what he had been doing. Still, the noises of his moving things, opening the drawer and shutting it briskly, opening the tap to let the running water set the scene, and the slow steps he took to open the door must have been audible to her on the other side. One look at his face, despite his attempts to wash it, was enough.

"I thought you had stopped," she said. She sounded different to me, as if she got cheated and taken for granted. She breathed hard and at any moment she could have shouted at him. She didn't because she seemed conscious of the people downstairs.

"I thought... " she paused, making an effort to restrain.

"Please let's not talk about this now. I am ready to go down," he said.

"Sit," she said firmly, putting her hands on his shoulders. "Just sit here, okay?" She made him sit at the edge of the bed and closed the bedroom door.

"Lock it, please—"

"Vishal, listen. I am not your enemy."

"I know."

"I can't shout. But I am worried."

"Don't be. This…" He sighed and looked at the wash-basin, "*This* was after a long time."

"You have no idea how much I am holding myself back. And yet you lie to me?"

"When?"

"Just now. This doesn't look like it was after a long time," she said.

"Why are you getting stressed?"

"This is so difficult, you know that? For all of us?"

"And for me."

"Is it? Do you love her? Do you want to marry her?"

"It's not easy. I don't want to cheat her."

"Then?"

"This is not deliberate. I am made to do this. It happens. I just have to."

"And you want it too?"

"Yes. I cannot be frank with anyone, except you."

"Then why do you expect her to marry you?"

Vishal kept staring at her.

"Why don't you join rehab?"

"No."

"What's so problematic about it?"

"It will end everything."

"This is going to end anyway," she said.

"Will she marry me if I join rehab? Tell me."

His aunt kept mum, maybe to avoid an instant reply.

"If I join rehab," he continued, "everyone will know at some point. This family, our relatives, this city has no concept of anonymity. The shame of it will shatter my parents, more than the knowledge of me taking drugs."

"They care about you."

"Much more about their reputation."

"But you will get better there. And, you know it."

"Please! Please let's go down."

"Vishal, you told me you had stopped. And you seemed well. I could see it. When I saw you and Divya getting closer... and through our conversations, I started believing you have actually stopped. I was a fool, wasn't I?"

"No, No—"

"We all have been fooled by your lies." She shook her head, looking stricken. "This is laughable. We need to be laughed at! What are we preparing for today? There is nothing special. This is dangerous for her, and your marriage."

"Please don't talk like you are not my friend."

"Well, I am. Being frank, now, is your only hope when it comes to Divya."

Vishal rocked on the bed, wanting to get up and leave. To walk down the stairs like nothing had happened. He fidgeted and hated what he heard. But he bit his lip. He was silenced. Choked. His eyes welled up. There were no more explanations to give. He looked at his friend with hope.

"Stop thinking." She took a deep breath. "Okay... let me put it this way. Maybe, this will sound easier for you." His aunt waited for a while to think of her response... and continued, "You step out now and behave as if nothing happened. Just be yourself. Okay? I am letting this stay hidden, but only for the next few hours. Do you get it? The condition is, you will tell her everything tonight or by tomorrow. Every little bit of this. You love her, right? Then stop cheating her. You can think through, analyse, do whatever you want. But, by tomorrow, you will tell her everything."

"Tell me what?"

Divya had gently pushed open the door, which was unlocked. She had waited downstairs for quite some time. She must have found it strange that he had not come to greet her. Maybe, she heard the entire conversation...

Seeing her, he stopped fidgeting. He gave up. Tears streamed down his eyes. And with his tears, I began to lose hope.

Someone had switched off the music *we* made in his head. We had stopped dancing. I felt it being stopped. Crushed. All the movement around me, everything that spun around me, that twisted us into a mass of chaos - it all stopped. Physiology took an unexpected beating from a foreign pressure. We didn't know what to do. We kept making futile attempts to pump out all possible ions from his cells. But his cells recoiled and his thoughts died down.

We had no choice but to slow down, sit back, and sleep.

That... was back then and now... at last, Vishal was feeling like he wanted to move out from here, from this place we hated as much, this place with people in white coats and the medicines that Divya sorted for him, thoughtfully.

We would wait. That seemed like the best option. Trapped inside him. Till the next time, he sat down to snort some more of our folks, and take them all in. Then he would re-live. And realize what he needed. We hoped he would try.

With Divya around, as it seemed, we could only... hope.

# A Healthy Home

The grey cobblestone alley in the remote village was flanked by huts on both sides. The huts had concrete walls, painted in dull brown or white. The alley was swept and washed. The identical grey square-shaped paving stones cushioned our laboured footsteps. It was nearly lunchtime and the aromas of pickles, cooking potatoes and onions wafted to our noses from the huts we passed.

But then our track cut off... from the alley into a broad path of dried mud in few shades of brown, with a scattering of grass and stones. The abrupt change almost seemed intentional. A wall, stood on one side of the path, having multiple rows of chiselled rectangular rocks of various sizes stacked together. A nauseous, dark-grey, sluggish liquid flowed in an open sewer below the wall, separating it from the path. Small vegetable farms occupied the other side. Adjoining the farms, we saw a couple of isolated huts about half a kilometer away. We were close to our destination. These huts had naked walls — exposed red bricks held together by fresh cement.

The walls had no dressing, no prepping and no sense of display. But someone had made a point of building them.

Why was I doing this? Why did I get up at six to travel four hours from the city to reach these remote villages, every day, six days a week?

There were twenty of us spread across ten villages. Our work involved taking interviews of mothers - women with children six to twelve months of age, to understand child feeding practices. We had to probe their difficulties in ensuring the best health and nutrition for their infants. We had to 'unlearn' what other researchers had documented over the previous decade, correct the misperceptions due to which malnutrition persisted in India. We hoped to obtain different insights and perspectives from mothers. Desk-based analysts at the main office in the city used an elaborate software to make sense of the data we gathered. Senior researchers published scholarly papers in reputed scientific journals based on our ground-work. These papers were supposed to influence health policy in India.

Was I disgruntled? Was that the right word? I couldn't help feeling our work was a massive exercise in pointlessness. Would it have any tangible impact on the immediate generation of babies that would be delivered, say next year, in this high-fertile region? Would it actually influence policy? And, why take interviews anyway? Our insights could be incomplete, but didn't we know enough about malnutrition and why it occurs? Shouldn't we first try to implement a few of our great ideas? Or maybe doing the actual work - to support every mother in every household of these ten villages - was too demanding or uninteresting? I didn't feel anger anymore. I was exhausted. No, that was on the surface! Helpless? No, not exactly - I had drafted my resignation email. Pathetic? Yes! Pathetic was the word for working with this team. Pathetic how we all carried on, thanks to the fat pay cheques we got from big funders. I loved my salary, but I hated the interviews. I didn't want to visit these homes. Not for the sake of some papers that would be written somewhere that would have no bearing on the lives of the people I met. At the end of the day, learning and unlearning helped us, and not the mothers. I wanted to help them. Assuming they needed it.

As we approached one of the huts with the naked red bricks, a woman stepped out with a beaming smile. She must have heard the sound of our shoes in the stifling silence of the afternoon. To her, it was natural to live in a secluded corner, divorced from the main village. She was dark and short with plaited hair. She looked young to be a mother. She wore a white *salwar* and a faded pink *kurta* with floral patterns of green and red.

Before my colleague or I could greet her, she said, "*Namaste.* Come in!"

"*Namaste Didi*", I said in Hindi. "Your name is Jyoti, right?"

"Yes, yes – Vimla, uh... Aanganwadi *didi*? She told us about you coming."

"Yes." I gave a small nod and a half-baked smile.

She rushed in and started tidying and arranging things.

I looked at Rachna, my colleague, and expected her to be annoyed, but she wasn't. She peered through the half-open creaking wooden door, as if to check where had Jyoti disappeared. But I took some effort to hold my nerves - Why couldn't these meetings ever be spontaneous? We kept telling the Aanganwadi workers - or the village health workers, not to make advance visits to the homes we wanted to survey. To not forewarn the mothers, much less tutor them on how to behave and what to say! A village-based government health worker should not end up colouring our data. Anyway, who cared!

Jyoti called us and we stepped in. The grey floor with crude uneven patches had a peculiar slant — the kitchen area on our right seemed a bit elevated, and it merged with the straight flattened track that led us to a room where we could see four chairs and a cupboard. There were two black goats on our left, busy chomping on a pile of grass inside a tiny partial enclosure also made of exposed brick. We had to watch our steps, to avoid stomping on a few tiny clay balls – their droppings scattered on the floor.

"Goats. But I... I will clean it now," she said, a bit hurriedly.

The kitchen was organized. She had washed and arranged the steel plates, cups and bowls in short vertical stacks. Indicating that we should proceed to the room, she continued to stir porridge on a pale black *chulha* with a heap of wooden sticks on the side. Moving towards the room, we saw an adjacent smaller room. Rachna went ahead and took a chair. I paused... to peek inside the smaller room. A man was sleeping on a bed in a diagonal posture, with head partly rested on a pillow, legs dangling out at the other end, and a thick green blanket covering his neck and torso. I could not guess his age, but he appeared older than Jyoti. He had that familiar stench - sickly, nasty and strong.

"Sir, I have a call from the office," Rachna called out.

"For me? Office?" I entered the room and took her phone.

"Hello!"

"Sir, your friend called from Geneva," said my other colleague at the office.

"What? Why?"

"Sir, wait, I will read his message for you…" There was a brief pause.

" 'Listen! The workshop went very well at the World Health Organization. Can't describe the feeling. Presentation applauded! A palatial conference room! Discussion went on all day and got intense. Reviewers are very excited. They will sanction phase-2 training support! By the way, the entire trip was funded. Business-class tickets. Loved it! And—' "

"Wait - where are you reading this from?"

"Sir, his WhatsApp message. First, he tried messaging you. But you have bad network there. So, he messaged me and asked me to call you, to convey."

"Great! I will read the remaining when I am back."

"Sir, which workshop?"

"Training on responsive child feeding in a rural low-income setting."

"That's interesting! Alright Sir, have a great day." He hung up. I handed the phone to Rachna.

"What happened?" she asked.

"Nothing. Will tell you later." I sat down and started taking out our material from my bag and placed it on the adjacent chair.

"Look at the baby boy and his sister!" she said.

I glanced to my right. Jyoti's young son was asleep on the bed, protected from flies and mosquitoes by an old net tacked to the wall with strings. We couldn't see his face. I was not sure if the net helped much. Resting on the bed, by his side, her older daughter was staring at us, maybe with a million little amorphous bubbling thoughts... about our faces, our artificial smiles, our clothes, our watches, our way of talking, our English whispers, our Hindi accents, our notebooks, our ball-pens, our audio-recorders and our shoulder bags, leather shoes and sandals. Jyoti was still scrubbing the floor after removing the goat-poop.

"Is he your brother?" Rachna tried to break the ice. The girl nodded with a blank face.

We were waiting in a small living room of sorts. It had a tube-light, a small bed, four modest wooden chairs kept in a line, and a short black steel cupboard. The walls were baby-pink. The floor was tiled. Only this room had a tiled floor. The white ceiling had a limited span. Right at its centre, a chocolate-brown fan churned the air lazily. The room had no specks of dirt and no cobwebs. A plastic shelf was nailed to the wall. It had an idol of Lord Ganesh and things like tablets, powder, combs and brushes, a few soft toys, a packet of *bindis* and some plastic bangles.

"*Beta*, where is *papa*?" I thought of breaking the ice too.

She didn't reply.

"Tell us...?" Rachna made an effort.

The girl pointed to the neighbouring room that had the sickly smell.

"So, wake him up. It's twelve, time to have lunch."

The girl didn't reply. I told Rachna to drop it.

Jyoti entered the room and sat on the floor, folding her legs.

"No, please take a chair, why are you sitting down?" I said, almost standing up.

"No, I like to. Don't worry. And soon, my boy will wake up. I will have to feed him. It's better to sit here and feed under the fan."

"Oh... okay." I paused to have a quick look at the questions in my notebook, and started:

"Tell us Jyoti, who all are there in your family?"

"My husband, my son and my daughter. And, my in-laws."

"Oh... where are they?"

"They have gone to the *Panchayat* office. They will be back in an hour."

I made a mental note to wind up within an hour. If her in-laws arrived, there would be no scope left to understand her thoughts and beliefs. She wouldn't open up in their presence.

"How old are your children?"

"My daughter is three years and son is ten months."

"And your age?"

"Twenty-four."

"So, your husband is sleeping there..."

"Yes." She smiled and quickly looked down to make an effort to adjust her *kurta* over her folded knees. She looked at Rachna and then, at her daughter. "He came home very late... in the morning. At four. I don't think he will wake up so soon."

"That's okay. I was just asking. We will talk to you."

She nodded.

"So, we have a form here—" I looked at the sheet of paper in my hand, "— it tells about our work and why we are visiting you. We want to understand your difficulties in feeding your child. We want your permission for the interview and need you to sign the form. And we have a recorder because, uh... it's easier... to understand what you tell us if we don't have to take notes and keep writing. I hope you are... okay with all of this?"

"Yes. Aanganwadi *didi* told me about these things."

Rachna read out the consent form explaining the confidentiality of the information that Jyoti would give us, and that she could withdraw from the interview at any time if she wanted to. After Jyoti signed it, we switched on the recorder.

We kickstarted the interview with standard questions. Our subject, a 24-year-old *Dalit* woman, was the sole breadwinner for a family of six people, with a daily wage of a hundred and twenty rupees, paid in irregular instalments, as one may expect for a landless farm labourer. Although she was promised three hundred. The adjoining vegetable farms suffered, thanks to the unpredictability of nature and strained access to irrigation. She made time to scrub and clean the floors and dishes in other homes, located in the better part of the village, just so she could get food for her children - things like biscuits, bananas and sometimes *laddoos*. She was often paid for these chores in kind, which was perhaps more useful than cash. Her in-laws were frail, and her husband worked on occasion. Alcohol had ravaged his health and productivity, and this led to erratic behaviour and verbal duels with farm owners. They used him only if *'no one else could make it'*. The challenges of her everyday existence were 'great data' for our analysis.

I switched over to questions related to her ten-month-old child: "After he was born, what did the nurse do?"

"She showed him to me, and everyone was happy. My husband, parents… they all wanted to have a look at him."

"So, what happened then?"

"The nurse took him away for some time, for cleaning. Then, the baby was held by my family members, my husband's brothers, their wives… everyone wanted to observe him, play with him. It took some time."

"How long?"

"An hour. Maybe longer. I started feeding after an hour."

"And, from that day till the time he was six months of age, have you only breastfed? I mean, nothing else?"

"No. How can that happen? Aanganwadi *didi* keeps telling us, but that's not possible in our home."

"Why?"

"Sometimes there are things we do. We have to do."

"Like?"

"Rituals."

"What kind of rituals?"

"Whenever there is any special day, the baby is given *ghutti* - that liquid, you know?"

I nodded.

"It is sacred. I can't stop our elders from doing that. They have been practising it for so many years…" She halted, to look at me as if to gauge my reaction.

"Yes, go on."

"And—" she stopped for a second, "— and, when the baby is sweating too much, they insist that I give him water…" She paused to take a breath. "In between, I was outside, working, and could not return for more than three hours. So, my mother-in-law fed him cow's milk. I got upset, but, I can't argue with her."

"Why?"

"Because she would have ridiculed me."

"In what way?"

"Saying that I am away for so long and she can't stand her grandson crying out of hunger."

"Okay... Did he fall ill during those first six months, I mean, things like loose motion, cough or fever?"

"No fever... but loose motion, yes. Many times. We gave him ORS. Aanganwadi *didi* has taught us."

"But you do know why he got ill?"

"The air is bad. We have a sewer outside. What else?"

"Do the babies in your neighbours' homes or elsewhere in the main village, get ill as often during those early months?"

She thought for a while, then shook her head. I probably shouldn't have asked that. She frowned.

"No, that doesn't happen. Are you saying that my child fell ill because he got other things to eat?"

"No, please don't take this as your fault alone."

"But it is. I am his mother. I should have been firm with other people."

"You were firm. You tried."

"Then why should he fall ill?"

I stopped for a moment to think of an answer. This was an interview and purely that. But she needed some clarity.

"Outside things should not be given." I said. "As much as possible. Not even water, not till six months are over.

See, your baby only knows your body. He has stayed inside you for nine months, lived on your blood. Hence, outside milk or water is... it is different, foreign, and something that his stomach is not used to. So, it reacts... and hence, loose motion."

"I think he is waking up," Rachna butted in.

We heard a suppressed cry. Jyoti rushed to the bed. She dismantled the net removing one string at a time, took him out, cuddled him and asked her daughter to place a cloth on the floor so he could crawl around after being fed. She turned his head and pointed to us, saying things like, 'Look who's here!' 'We have guests to meet you!' 'Say *Namaste!*'

"I think you should just stick to asking questions. If you advise, we won't get unbiased data," Rachna muttered while fiddling with the recorder.

"I will. But after a point, we will switch it off." I said, eyeing the recorder.

"Why?"

"I don't know. I think we should get data while we... just converse with her. Don't you see? This set-up isn't making her comfortable, although she won't say that to us."

Soon, the mother and her baby joined us and sat down on the makeshift cloth mat with frayed edges, oozing excitement and looking at us with glittering smiles that masked the distressing situation in their home. In him, Jyoti could forget her routine and its gravity.

"He is my son. Arjun. Very naughty! And he doesn't want to eat!"

"Oh, is it!" My questions had to be tweaked. "So, tell me why he won't?"

"I don't know, ask him!" she smiled.

"Why don't you eat Arjun?" I played along. The baby gurgled at me. "What do you feed him usually?"

"Whatever is available. Or whatever I can get from others' homes."

"What has Aanganwadi *didi* advised you?"

"*Suji ki kheer*, *khichri*, *dal*, boiled potatoes... she said I can mash them together."

"And are you able to give all this?"

"Yes. But he gets cranky. Refuses to eat. He has been cranky since the time we started attempting to give all this, four months back."

"After six months of age - is that when you started...?"

"Yes —" she held back to think. "No, later... after the seventh month."

"Okay. Why do you think he gets cranky?" I asked.

"I don't know. All babies do. They don't want to eat."

"Hmm... is that what you think?"

"Why could it be?" She lowered her voice.

"We just spoke about it," I smiled. "The child... I mean, any child, when he gets outside things right from the beginning, when he should get mother's milk only, is not prepared... I mean he can't take things like *kheer* and *khichdi*, at the right age."

"But..." she paused a bit, "is that the reason?"

"You don't think so?"

"I think, children are so little. They just can't eat everything that we want them to eat. These are the things that big people like us eat easily. But he is only ten months old."

"Yeah."

"He doesn't even know why he is eating all that", she said.

"So… you do see that babies are so little. Such little tummies. Such new foods." I smiled.

She looked at me as if she bore the weight of those words. But she didn't seem to agree.

I pushed it a little – "I mean, do you see that new foods are difficult – I mean, anything new? Like something that is not mother's milk during the early days. That's also… new… right?"

"No…" she nodded. "I don't think that's the reason that he is not eating now."

"Then why do you think this is happening?"

"uh… I don't know, but are we responsible for this – that he fusses and doesn't eat now?"

"No, no… leave that aside. Don't take the blame."

"But it has changed his body, his habits, as you say," she looked at Arjun. "And, he is fussing as we can see. So…"

"Yeah?"

"So… it needs to be fixed. How can I solve this?"

"Well… you try every day. Every day with your child is another day you learn, you try, you observe and spot something."

"How?"

"Okay..." I sighed. "Let's try something now..." I had to restrain myself as I was getting recorded. "So tell me... how often do you feed him?"

"Twice, or sometimes thrice. He only takes half of a *katori*."

"Do you know how much he needs to take for his age?"

"Four or five times a day is what Aanganwadi *didi* said."

"What else did she tell you?"

"Give bananas, apples if possible. Give something sweet, but home-cooked. Not the biscuits that you get from others' homes. Give a lot of vegetables..."

She continued. "I have tried some of these things. But I have to serve four other people and then eat myself. If I don't eat well, how will I feed him —"

"Wait... you still feed him?"

"Yes, he must have my milk! Else he will fall sick. He hardly eats *khichri* or other things. And she said five times a day! Even once or twice, half a *katori* is a big task. I must feed him my milk. And... how can I spend on fruits?"

My God! What was that all about? Could we pinpoint only on the lack of money? Was it the knowledge - the tragedy of not getting the right advice at the right time. But it was unfair to say that incorrect beliefs set the rules. Weren't there other families who had realized that breastmilk is the best in the initial months? Weren't they cutting down on foreign liquids? Weren't they becoming aware? Flexible with their beliefs? Why not her? Because she was a *Dalit*? The little information that trickled down to her, *via* the health worker, neighbours and the village as a whole, was too superficial to process and too limited to bring about any change in her thinking, let alone her family's. Workers needed to converse with them. People needed to sit down and talk to the in-laws and elderly, perhaps right from the time of pregnancy. Yes, bananas were expensive; but had it even registered that a variety of food items would only add to her son's chances of eating more? And what could we do when they simply could not afford it?

While I was lost in my thoughts, sifting through the pages of my notebook for no reason, Rachna asked if she should switch off the recorder. I nodded. Meanwhile, Jyoti had left the scene. A minute later, she brought a bowl of porridge from the kitchen and started feeding her son.

"Now, look what he does..." She brought my attention to the spoon.

The child took two spoons and seemed fine. At the third, he squirmed. He tried to move around. He crawled towards the bed. He crawled to our feet and tried to climb into my bag lying on the floor. He did whatever he could to stay away from the spoon. He had learned to make his life's first set of excuses before learning to eat.

Jyoti made him sit on her lap and fed one more spoon. The child looked at my bag and let the spoon slip in his mouth. She had to make an effort to slip it in. For the next spoon, he furrowed his brow. For the next, he pursed his lips.

"See?"

"Yeah."

"Every time, the same thing," she said.

"Hmm..."

"What do I do?"

"Do you want to change the colour?"

"What?" She looked at me, her expressionless face almost wanted to give up.

"Why?" Rachna butted in, trying to figure out what I was getting at.

"Do you have spinach?" Flashes of some green vegetables I had noticed in her kitchen came to my mind.

"No...yes... uh... a little... but my neighbour may have more of it."

"Can you bring it?"

"He won't eat spinach."

"No, no... just use some of it, boil it first and then mash it a little, mix it with the porridge. And stir well."

She looked at Rachna for any tinge of second opinion. Rachna nodded, but with a doubtful glare towards the child. Jyoti handed the child over to her daughter's care. She went out and vanished for a full fifteen minutes.

"Just wait," I told Rachna.

When she was back, the porridge, which she had re-warmed a little, had taken a different texture. A gentle greenish hue mixed with light yellow. She sat down to make a fresh attempt.

"Arjun... come here, come here... look what we have! Look!"

Arjun gazed at the variegated yellow-green meal, throwing a few vapours in the air. For a moment, nothing distracted him from his play. After it had cooled down a bit and she had lured him enough with loud animated calls, she started feeding him. He looked at the spoon for a little while, and chewed on it, slowly. He made a face as if he was testing it. He stared at her and she didn't drop her smile. When he was done chewing, she fed him another spoon. He took it. And another. And, he took one more. Her attempts got more energized. She babbled to mimic his voice. She sensed his moods. He chewed on. He licked his lips. At times, he too babbled to her calls. She carried on - she tweaked his name and cooed to him, and he smiled at her. Yes, he did crawl to our feet and tried to get into our bags, but this time with a bit of smiling, gurgling and hand flapping! She pulled him gently and fed him another spoon. He took two more. She laughed in disbelief, and he could only look in wonder, hearing her laugh! Her daughter joined the party and fed him two more spoons. Arjun loved the change of hands... or, probably the spinach... or, just the things happening, as a whole...Who could say?

"Have you done this before?" I probed.

"Umm... No, not in this way... I mean, I thought he won't like it. And, we don't *do* this."

"Do what?"

"The spinach. No one told me. My mother-in-law may not know. Let's see what she says."

"She may not agree?" I asked.

"It's hard. She will say, '*why this effort*'. And—" Jyoti stopped herself to frame what she wanted to say. "But I will talk to her. These are new things."

"Yes, new things... but they will help you. They aren't that difficult, right?"

"Yes. Spinach."

"No, it's not about the spinach."

"Then?"

"What I want to say is... you know him well, but there are things you can't be sure of. He is yours. But he is also a different *person*. He has his tastes. And his tastes are building now."

"Okay." She looked at the *katori* with more than half of its meal eaten, and it seemed like she got lost in thought.

"So, try whatever you can to make it interesting for him. What do you think?"

"Yes. I will try - maybe this spinach, now.... and again after some days."

"Yes, but... I mean, keep changing your ways. Today it is spinach, tomorrow it could be a carrot, boiled and mashed with that gentle orange hue. Someday, it could be beetroot... boiled and mashed giving that strong red colour. Right? One day, it could even be *dal,* so that the dark yellow gets mixed with the white *kheer*. Sometimes you could try putting nuts, in the centre of the *kheer.* If you can get those from somewhere. So he sees those brown dots. If possible, try a fruit... I mean... only if possible." I smiled.

"Hmm..."

"I know it's hard."

"What if my mother-in-law stops me from trying this out?"

"She might. But she wants a grandson that grows stronger. Remember – you *both* want him to eat, you both want him to eat more and eat happily. Right? So, talk to her."

"Okay," she looked at Arjun, clinging onto her, trying to say something. Calling her and cooing at her. "I just...

never thought this. These different things. I mean, we have never done it." She smiled, looking at her older daughter.

"I know. But children love different things. They are figuring out what they like. It's not just a confused tummy that got outside milk and water at the wrong times… and now it's fussy and rejects the same old *kheer* and *khichri* fed twice or thrice a day. It's also a confused mind, yours and his."

She heard that intently, while I thought if I should stop. "So… just keep trying other things," I said.

"Yes." She nodded, still staring at her child, still in awe. Arjun had nearly finished the *katori*. Her attention swung between the ideas I threw at her, and her child's euphoria.

It was time to leave. We began to pack our stuff. As we stepped out of the room, I peeped into the adjacent room. Her husband was still asleep. The sickly smell had dimmed. The kitchen was a bit cluttered due to the spinach. The *chulha* had stopped burning. The goats had quietened. The fodder was eaten. The floor was clean. The red bricks displayed the self-esteem of a *pucca* house. She left Arjun to play with his sister and accompanied us to the door. We stepped out of her house. The familiar path that greeted her, the dried mud, the open sewer, and the stone wall right in front, had nowhere else to go. Her work would remain the same. Her wages would not rise. Her troubles would not cease. Raising a cranky, physically weak child with a 'confused mind and tummy' in a restricted home rooted in beliefs and disconnected from newer ideas, was no child's play. No one had impacted her. Not the health worker. Not her advice of *'eat this, eat that… feed five times.'* Not her family. Not her detached village. Not those relatives who got excited about the birth of a male child. And, not us. Not our interview. Not our research and analysis. Not the prescriptions of the World Health Organization. I left her and walked ahead, trying to process my thoughts.

As Rachna held her hand and took her leave, she said, "He never ate a full *katori* for the past four months. I still don't believe he did it."

# Not in the Dark

The knife slashed the front of her elbow. The grey, shining, serrated edge of the metal cut through her skin, making a dark red slant. Without a hint, the wound started to gape a little... and then a bit wider, tearing the skin apart. A current of bright red liquid poured out and fell vigorously onto the floor. Her eyes stared at me, threatening to hit back. Those intense, plunging, arresting eyes. Shell-shocked as they were, they looked ready to scream. As I watched, her shoulder drooped to her right, she doubled over and her knees folded. Before I could hold her, she fell on her arm with a thud. Her bangles clanked hard as they hit the floor. She lay on her side, motionless with her face fixed at me. Her eyes were half-open, gazing at my shoes. Her breathing stayed on. Slow. Weak. Stopping in between. Resuming. Persisting. Fragmented - like a slow shiver. Her right arm was outstretched, her fingers still seemed to move.

Blood had spattered onto the clean white floor, making a pool under her right elbow. Red trails began - fat fresh trails that branched from one to many, making faltering lines through curved bends, like reckless tributaries going berserk, routing and turning the way they wanted. Some inched closer towards me. Some raced up to the wall and crashed against it.

After a while... the bleeding seemed to lessen, and the pool under her elbow blackened, turning darker with each passing minute. The stench had become unbearable. She breathed slowly for a few minutes... and her eyes began to close. She went to sleep.

I let out a slow sigh of relief, which *he* interrupted. When had I let him in?

Saket was recruited as Head of Operations, a little more than a year ago, by her... she who now lay there. He was a bright chap... ideating, thinking beyond the workings, and her man Friday. It was a perfect match: the industrious, strategic, ideating manager met the driven, ambitious, visionary founder.

"Why did you do this?" he asked me. His brow was tense and wrinkled. He looked straight into my eyes as he gently seated himself on the sofa.

"She asked for it," I said, and went to sit on the armchair opposite him.

"Let me help you," he said.

"No."

"Drop the knife!" He arched forward as if to snatch it away.

"No," I said.

"Why?"

"I don't trust you." I shifted in my chair.

"Why?"

"Who can trust you?" I said, my face twitching.

"You don't have to," he said. "Just drop the knife."

"I need it."

"Why?" he yelled.

"For my sake!" I yelled back.

His voice slowed down, became softer. "I am not the one with a weapon, Rohit."

His voice remained familiar. A husky, menacing tone. Always defensive. Argumentative. Holding to his position. Questioning my line of thought. Trying to prove me wrong. Pointing towards me, that I was the one with the problem.

His voice remained familiar. His ways too. Like the first time… a month after his joining. On an occasion that looked like a regular office party.

……………………………

The first time, *they* hid themselves. Or almost. Behind the people. Behind the dozen-odd dancing couples. Behind large white circular tables flanked by tall brown chairs. Behind the towering flower-vases that stood on the centres of the tables. Behind the hundred heads and faces, laughs and jokes, and the banter and chatter, which cut them off from the rest of us. From me.

I strolled on the other side of the rectangular hall, keeping close to the wall, sneakily and intermittently trying to grab a closer view. They had skipped the tables, settling for a couple of isolated maroon chairs with black legs, to snuggle up against the opposite wall. I watched as they chatted with keen eyes, holding finely tapered champagne flutes filled with the seductive golden drink. The glasses clinked—in between—a few times, for some precious dedications that had to be made. They ensured that they sat next to the horrendously head-splitting DJ, so that they could hardly hear each other's voices, and went on laughing and giggling at half-heard, half-baked jokes. I didn't want to interrupt. No questioning. No confrontation. No scenes to be created!

Watching them gave me a sense of awakening that something like this could happen right before my eyes. From what I could figure, he would tell her an anecdote, whispering into her ears. Then he would ask her something. She would nod, then purse her lips to indicate that she had no clue. He would persist. Ask her again. She would give up. Then, he would burst out with what seemed to be the unbelievable answer. She would almost spill her wine, laughing at his remark and smothering her mouth with her palm. He would gaze at her while she laughed, using every moment it seemed, to cherish her. When she calmed down, she would look at him for a while. She appeared almost grateful that he could do that to her—make her laugh. Their eyes would meet for a split-second. And she would roll her eyes back at the dancing couples, to break the eye contact. She would blush a little, smile at him as his gaze fixed on her. And, he would take his next sip. They had no idea I was there, watching.

Watching Saket with Arti... his boss, the one who had given him a platform to grow, via her company, the one who trusted him completely. Arti, my wife.

..................................

I shifted once more in the chair. "You just want to be a yes-man to her, till you slowly trap her in your larger plan..." I told Saket.

"What? What do you mean?"

"You are luring her."

"I like Arti, I respect her," he asserted.

"Complete it."

"Yes, I am attracted to her. Perhaps, I love her."

"It doesn't suit you."

"Don't be rude!"

"Don't you have any shame?"

"After what you have done to her now?" Saket stared at the knife, while wiping the sweat that trickled down the side of his face.

"She's alive."

"She's bleeding."

"If you love her, why don't you help?" I asked him.

"Stop brandishing the knife and I will."

"You do care for your survival, don't you?"

"Rohit, we all do. Look at her. She does too."

Then I had to say it. "You broke up my home."

He lowered his head… and took a deep breath. He seemed to gather his thoughts to pick the right words. He looked at Arti. "Did you have a home?" he said, but avoided looking at me.

"I had Arti. Our routines. A few conversations. A few dinners. We had something. A piece of life. Until she met you."

"*We* - we met. You always forget that. She never stopped me."

"She didn't fully understand."

"And *you* did?" He glared at me. "That's why she lies on the floor? You are a freak, Rohit."

"Call me that or anything. You can't provoke me. I did what I had to."

"Then drop the knife."

I gripped it and swallowed hard. "If I do, would you take her to the hospital?"

"*We* would."

"Why would we? Why do we need you with us, in any way?"

"Fine, you take her. I will leave after you call the ambulance."

"Only to be asked questions by the doctors, the police and by Arti herself? You really think I am a freak?" I waved the knife to push him back, so he could stay away a little. I hated the way he leaned forward, staring at me and probing deep into my statements.

"Are you going to let her die?" Saket squirmed in his seat, looking at Arti - she appeared to be more still, more detached than some time back... when he had rung the doorbell, only to be greeted by my sweaty face and blood dripping from the knife.

"She won't die," I said. "Look at the place where I cut her... nothing will happen. Have some sense." I smiled at him.

I wanted him to leave our home without worrying about her. I wanted him to be as detached, as she had become, in the last few months, with me.

"Tell me Saket, why did you guys, at the party, I mean— the first time— assume that people would not spot the obvious?" I threw the question and he stared at me.

"What do you mean?"

"The way you both were talking to each other."

"But you weren't there… how do you know?"

"How do you know I was not there?"

"It was an office party. She threw it. It had our team and some business partners. When did you come?"

"I was always there. She didn't know. That explains why she felt so free with you. I turned up two hours into the party, by the time the glasses were refilled, the dances became maddening, and the music became noise."

"Why didn't you meet us?" He formed creases on his brow.

"I didn't want to. I wanted to observe."

"We were drinking and chatting and that's about it. For God's sake, I report to her. That's the way it started. And, that's the way it is. Still. We eat, drink and work long hours, almost seven days a week."

"And so?" I asked.

"As in?"

I glared at him, waiting for him to speak more.

"That's how we are, Rohit." He sniffed, as if to buy time to gather the words. "And one day, our office anniversary date pops out of nowhere. We didn't even sense it was coming. We needed a break. We surely deserved to laugh. There's nothing wrong about that. And you thought I was…" he paused.

"You always wanted that and you got it. It was your first step. Right from the day she hired you."

Saket widened his eyes, as though astonished, but held back an answer. How could he defend himself anyway? He could defend facts. Not motives, those that stared through his eyes. He let out a deep sigh. He looked at Arti, and the spattered blood. He shook his head in disbelief. He squirmed a bit and finally slouched on the sofa. He kept looking at her but it seemed as if he had given up.

And I could only see, looking at him, a replay of the second time I had seen them together.

...............................

We had packed our luggage—mud-brown and sky-blue roller-bags. Our really old, favourite bags. It was for a one-night trip to a scenic valley of flowers. Arti, her team of four managers including Saket, and a bunch of other staff members had planned the day.

After breakfast, we stepped onto a majestic plain overlooking the valley. Our walking paths were narrow, flanked by vast swathes of bright rich purple orchids and lush green shrubs. We walked on these paths, stomping on dead grass and dried soil. We moved in small groups, often in pairs, changing companions fluidly, with some people moving ahead, and others slowing down. Gusts of cold air lashed my face. The large expanse of swaying flowers under a big blue sky seemed to grant us... freedom - a space unknown - and license the multiple changes of partners and conversations.

People walked alone, walked in pairs, walked apart. Their pace was hard to follow. I would find myself with one of her managers suddenly walking next to me, asking me how I was doing, how did it feel to work from home every day - you know, people showing me their pretentious appreciation, because I got to manage a lot 'sitting on my couch' and the like. Another one would join me only to praise Arti's many successes: her post-marital meteoric rise in her late-30s - that she chased her heart to conceive a design firm, lead it, diversify her expertise, and gain a slow, sure and immense respect in the corporate world. That she had done all this after getting married at 33 to a freelancer like me, dealing with his own struggles. She had succeeded despite his health taking a toll on her, despite the loneliness of success, despite her aggressive competitors, despite... well, it went on and on.

Her firm had expanded at a breakneck speed. Three years ago, it opened its first outlet in a couple of malls in Mumbai, finally stepping out of the digital space. A little more than a year ago, a rich industrialist bought a 10% stake for about a hundred crores and her current annual revenue stood at three hundred.

"Hard to imagine that, right?" Her head of finance had appeared out of nowhere to walk beside me. Was he right behind me when I got lost in my thoughts, or did he speed up to come closer, so he could pull me over for a chat?

"Rohit?" he called again. "What do you say?"

What did he expect me to say? "Yes. Yes, absolutely. Hard to imagine. Who would have thought!" I said. I kept wondering at her journey, and mine.

"I somehow believed in her when I joined this company," he said.

"Perhaps you believed in her more than I did."

We shared a momentary giggle, and he moved ahead. These men were coming to me and telling me things. Just to approach, say their bit and leave... trying to gauge what I felt about them, if I cultivated any envy, insecurity, discomfort, or a silent restlessness deep within; if they could pick on any one symptom, which they could scan. Asking me generic questions on how I was doing... they hardly wanted to know the roots of my suffering.

..................................

Arti and I are ten years apart. I am ten years older, now 48. Saket and Arti matched in not only their age, but also their home town (both hail from Pune). They also had similar taste in the arts: Haruki Murakami, old Marathi theatre, ghazals and European cinema. Stuff that appeared obscure and impenetrable to my mind, despite my best intentions and efforts. Even the choice of visiting a valley of flowers was theirs.

"What can I do? You know Saket by now. He knows how to convince," she had told me after we packed our bags, mud-brown and sky-blue, our really old favourite bags.

"Oh, *he* sure does."

"Don't strain yourself. Do you want to stay at home?" she asked me.

"Why don't you say if we should stay at home?"

"I can't. Even if I want to. Because it's planned."

"At least tell me that you feel like cancelling it."

She didn't reply. She adjusted her scarf. The knot didn't seem right.

"Rohit, did you pack your meds?" She began to untie the scarf.

"Why did you ask that?"

"I am just checking."

"No, you are not."

She kept mum for a second and said, "Okay. Because I get worried. If you want to know the truth."

"Or because we are not going alone and there are others… your team?"

"Rohit?"

"Seriously, you are worried about the public?"

"No." She knotted her scarf again. Looking straight at me, she said, "And, you know that. There is no pity. Not in my mind. Not in anyone's. They know it, but we don't discuss it. There is some respect to that, Rohit. Please."

"They ask me questions as if I am unwell."

"They ask out of concern. And they hardly know the details."

"Does he know the details?"

"Did I mention him?"

"No."

"Do I mention him?"

I did not respond.

"Now, tell me, have you packed your medicines?"

"Yes."

"Thank you," she blurted, went past the door in a second, and entered the elevator.

Such had been our routine conversations for more than a year. Terse. Pointed. Closing. And they overlapped with her growing interaction with Saket. I was left to carry on with 'my work', stabilize, calm myself down, and stop comparing my situation with the people I knew closely. Accept it for what it meant. Not think too hard… Love myself. Basically, stay happy. The sort of words that shaped our - well, the other kinds of conversations we had, which seemed to have more meaning.

...............................

So... *They* walked longer in the green and beige paths of dead grass and dried soil, flanked by purple orchids. The other groups were fairly typical - chattering about nature, the thin cold air and its rarity in a city like Mumbai. But, they walked longer... next to each other but keeping a little distance, in the narrow alley-like paths, and on the bumpy ones. Not that they didn't change partners. They did. A couple of times. Other people came, joined in and moved ahead. They did switch their conversations. But it was an Act. A pattern to show a picture of normalcy. For all of us. For me. I was walking a few feet behind, watching them. When they walked together, she zoomed out of her thinking mode to talk about the purple orchids. Arti talking about flowers was the most unlikely thing! No, it was not one of their common tastes in the visual arts, or anything of that sort. It was random. A conversation-starter. She would point to an orchid, describe it a little, and he would grab the opportunity to build onto her remarks. She would speak of its silence, its untouchable charm. How it could remain still and yet speak. Saket would deftly link these remarks with the long silences in *their* lives, their own lives, buried within the daily noise— saying how starved they had become, unable to travel and explore, simply to recover or to breathe in these spaces. How consumed they had become in their work to proudly declare themselves as workaholics, and achieving workaholics— to the point that they got little time to look after themselves. Why they found it difficult to cherish the making of a friendship— their brooding friendship— and forget that it was unusual, or strange, unconventional, and so unexpected at such a stage of their lives. And how afraid they had become to break down in any way imaginable, the extreme levels of self-consciousness that hindered them.

But I wanted to break the silence, the silence within my lungs, stuffed with pure, unadulterated, almost sweetened cold air from the valley. They had paced up a little and gone several feet ahead. I wanted to axe through their silence that made me want to scream.

Instead, I shouted out loud, a question: "Why did you join her company?"

They turned back. Arti's face turned pale, stern and expressionless. Saket, as if puzzled by the question, looked at her and back at me.

After a while, he shouted, "Rohit? You are asking me?"

"Yes. You both are ahead of me. And she is the founder."

"Yeah", he said.

"So the question is for you."

His face remained puzzled. After a brief lull, he said, "Well, Rohit, like any other person would join, right? For growth?"

"But why this company? You are an Operations Head. Such a dynamic, versatile portfolio. You can go anywhere. Maybe get more money. Why here?"

"All of this is on record with HR. The interview forms, yeah?"

Arti seemed to have given up by this time. She closed her eyes, breathing in and out gently, and just stood there.

"No, not the forms. I want to hear from you," I said.

"No Rohit. Not the right time."

"There is no one behind me. Everyone has gone ahead. You can tell me."

"It's not about them."

"Then? Just tell me."

He sighed, folded his hands and pressed his fingers into his waist.

I took a deep breath and blurted out, "Okay, if you won't, then let me explain - You have a history of two failed start-ups, your failed dreams that took a toll on you. The failure of your motivation. You've spent a good deal of your 20s, through the mid-30s, struggling and learning through setbacks. You wanted a platform—a ready platform that could put you on the map and get you some recognition. To leverage for bigger gains, monetary and otherwise, because clearly, you didn't have it in you to achieve success derived from your ideas. You needed someone else's ready vehicle. So, you researched. You read about people. You read about Arti and her work. How she worked hard. And got lucky at times, yes. Three years of ad-hoc work. But money poured in, while she managed and managed things. You scanned this company inside out. Then convinced her in the interview that she badly needed an Operations Head for a streamlined working model. That she needed You. Then you saw us, you noted our lives..."

"Rohit, hold on..." he said.

I didn't stop. "How difficult we were becoming for each other. In spite of love. How we were suffocating it, unknowingly. I, with my condition, our age-gap, our gaping professional differences. That we had no children – and, we may not have. It was the perfect recipe. This company has no natural co-head, co-partner. And there she is, Arti—she keeps thinking! The problem of having a vision, you know? She thinks ahead, ten years, fifteen years. She has no answers. Her firm... really... has no one, other than her! No match for her. It needs the other half of the brain."

"Rohit, wait..."

"And... that's how you came in. You hardly came as a sincere enthusiast. You hardly came as someone wanting to contribute. You came with an interest. A deep interest, almost as sustained as her vision for the company."

"Rohit, look at her."

"And you grew your influence as you had planned."

"See her!"

"To the point, that now you speak of being her friend. And she speaks of that too. And the times you both share. For all to see. Right before me."

"She is *bleeding*."


Bleeding.


That word brought me back to the scene— the blood, the marks, the trails. I was back at home, with Arti. Her breathing had slowed down. The eyelids had closed.

"Do you want to tell me what happened?" Saket asked.

"What...What happened?" I asked him.

"Why did you go on that rant?"

"It was no rant. I know you. I wish she knew you as much," I said.

He closed his eyes and inhaled as if to control an impulsive reply. He straightened on the sofa. And, it seemed that he changed the track of our conversation: "What exactly happened between both of you that you had to hurt her?"

"Why should I tell you?"

"Please let's call the ambulance. I am worried. Can I?" He got up, slowly, keeping a distance from me, and went near the body. He shook her a bit, called out her name, and looked at her neck and her chest to see any signs of breathing.

I said, "Only if this knife is wiped off my prints and placed back in her hand."

"What?"

"I am not answering anything to anyone. This is an accident."

"Okay," he paused to catch a breath. "Okay, if that's what it takes to help her."

"It has always been about helping her, hasn't it?"

"Look, Rohit—"

"It made her feel better that *I am well*, it always did. It helped her. And it had become my job to keep ensuring her, that I was well... so she could get on with her routine and her life."

I stood up. They had dried - no more red drops fell from the knife's edge. While he watched me get up and move, wary of the knife, I took a few steps ahead into the passage that connected the living room with our kitchen.

"We were arguing there, in the beginning," I said, pointing to a utensil rack, and went further inside the kitchen to open the top drawer. "She was packing her lunchbox. Salad. She was making it. It was one of our usual morning duels, the little tugs-of-war."

I pointed to the tools in the drawer. "This is where the knife came from."

I found myself next to the kitchen counter. I could not see him anymore, but I was loud enough for him to know.

"Rohit, leave that now, I am calling the ambulance," I heard him.

"Yes, but let me tell you what happened…"

………………………………

Our trip to the valley of flowers had been a month ago, yet I couldn't take it out of my head. None of those images left me. Not just Arti and Saket, but the images that bounced on me. Of what they could be indulging in, when I wasn't around. The stuff that others in her office joked about, and yet I couldn't figure or wasn't aware of. The little details that escaped me. Every morning when I saw her making breakfast, it hit me like a slap on the face… the trip, their equation, everything. And today was no exception.

She was busy slicing the cucumber. I was standing next to her. I looked at her intently. Then I asked, "Why do you guys gel with each other?"

"What kind of a question is that?" she said, continuing to slice the cucumber. She always liked the slices wafer-thin.

"Because the gelling happens with no one else."

"And yet, what does it prove?"

"Arti, there are ten other people... men... in your office—"

"And they are different people. Different roles, natures."

"Exactly."

"It proves nothing, Rohit."

"Don't get technical. Just tell me, why this friendliness with him?"

She raised her voice, and the slicing speed. "What is so wrong if we are friendly? Think about it, what is so wrong?"

"Where were you when we reached the end of the plain?" I asked.

"You all were having a little camp at its edge, at the fencing? Remember?"

"Yes. Don't act." I said.

"I was at the lake. I had told you. The right turn that came before. I took the detour."

"Yes, but you didn't wait for me. You went ahead with him."

"You said you will not come. You were not interested."

"And the others?"

"Rohit, they wanted to camp, sit for a while. And they were too tired."

"No, they were giggling on their way. They wanted to give you guys some space. They smiled at me. Mocked me. They thought I was a fool to even come for this trip."

"How do you know that?" she asked.

"I returned with them, without you. So I know."

"Rohit - how do you know what they were thinking about you?"

"I am your husband. He is your colleague. You guys hang out in private, with the others deserting you. And because I supposedly told you I won't come, you just go ahead with him. Who does that?"

She didn't answer.

"Why did it take till 8 pm for you to reach the hotel?"

"I reached by six. I was at the spa."

"And he joined you there? Did he?"

She didn't answer.

"He was not in his room. I checked," I said.

"You went to someone's room, to check?"

"Yes, how else should I contact you in that place with no network?"

"I told you, I would go to the spa, and be with you after I was done."

"So?"

"So why couldn't you just wait?" she asked.

"I am tired of waiting." I snatched the knife from her. She briskly let it go, lifted both her hands to escape a scratch and pushed herself back. I rushed off to the living room. She saw something familiar. Something we had done before. Something she thought she could handle. She moved towards me with uncanny speed but held herself back. She got closer, tried to grab the knife from my hand. I played it in the air to dodge her fingers. She took a step back but stretched out her right hand. It tremored a little.

"Give that to me," she said.

"No."

"Give it. Look, look…" She signalled with her palms. "Let me explain. You haven't heard me fully. You know that?"

"You make your plans. I agree with them. And you go ahead."

"Not true."

"You let him join you."

"No… No…"

"You grab the change you seek."

"No!" she yelled.

"That's what you have become."

"But, we will change it. We will change it, yeah?" she said.

"No, you are controlling me. You love these plans. You love it. You hardly want to change it." I brandished the knife over my arm, the shiny serrated edge barely sweeping its surface.

"Please… please drop it," her voice got heavier, her eyes welled.

"No."

"Drop it. Stop looking at it. Just drop it. Look at me - Rohit, look at me?"

"How can I trust you?" I waved the knife in between us, to keep her away.

"You don't have to. Just drop it."

"No."

"He will be coming any moment now."

"What?"

"Yes, we both wanted to talk to you. We wanted to make it clear. Not keep you in the dark anymore."

I heard that and pulled my hand down. What did she say?

I looked at her, into those plunging eyes. A nerve cracked in my head. What was that? That I had to be *explained* something. Not kept in the dark. I had to be awakened? He was coming here. What did *they* have to declare? And why, together? This was our home. Why him?

I swept the knife away from my trunk, slicing the air, and waved it towards her arm. She tried to stop me... but came in the way. The metal struck her... slashed the front of her elbow. The grey, shining, serrated edge cut through her skin, making a dark red slant. Without a hint, the wound started to gape, a little... and then a bit wider, tearing the skin apart...

............................

Who was I talking to? And why such details?

I had recounted the whole sequence of events to someone like Saket who I never trusted.

"Why did you come here?" I screamed, holding the bloodied knife, tapping it on the kitchen table.

He didn't answer.

"Hello?"

He stayed quiet. I didn't hear him calling the ambulance.

"Saket?"

No answer.

"What was it that you guys wanted to tell me?"

No answer.

"Saket?"

I wanted to check if he was still there in the living room. I stepped out. He wasn't there. I looked at her. She was asleep. The door was closed. I opened it, to check the outside door. It was closed too. Just the way I had kept it. Locked. Soon after she had fallen. She was still asleep. She seemed so, with the slow breathing. The lazy rise of the chest and its sinking back…

White waves flashed before my eyes. Out of nowhere. Chattering, screaming waves that crashed hard against towering, black rocks. They banged against stone, fell down and collapsed. And merged with the dirt, the silt, and the muddy waters sucked by the wasted green moss at the base of the rocks. The white waves dissolved into these, and lost their form, their life.

It had killed us… this one moment of weakness. The moment when I lost all my faith in her, my control on my impulse, and my grip on the knife.

When the danger we thought to our relationship—that person, he had vanished.

I heard the doorbell. Who was it? Saket? The ambulance? How did they know? Did they have something to tell me?

My head gave no more sounds, no more images. There were no more flashes. No couples dancing. No two people hiding in a noisy party, no two friends sharing whispers, jokes, smiles and blushes. No two people sitting in a corner snuggling up to a wall. No walking in pairs on narrow paths, next to purple orchids. No silences shared between them. I didn't see any of it. I could only see her, now... with her eyes closed, soaked in a red fluid, losing its darkness and the harshness of its smell. The red trails faded... on the clean white floor and vanished into the white wall. The fingers seemed to move, one after the other. The broken breaths joined together, to form a sort of rhythm. The few bits of energies that she gathered up... Her head moved a bit. The eyes rolled a little and the eyelids opened. She looked at me. She wanted to explain. Not keep me in the dark. She began to wake up. And I —

Was I awake?

# A Frantic Call

At 1 am, before she closed her eyes, Neha asked me the dreaded question:

"Where's Daddy?"

I held her small joined fists that had pulled up the white blanket and said, "He is at work… still, at work."

"He didn't call," she said.

"Hmm." I nodded.

"Why didn't he call?"

"I don't know."

She didn't blink. She kept staring. Her eyes piercing at mine.

"He must be very busy," I added.

She took a breath and loosened her grasp on her grey grizzly bear. Before she could let it slip, I said:

"He's trying to sleep. Hold him!"

She didn't answer. I made her fingers slide over the bear's trunk.

"Daddy must be really busy. He loves you very much."

She did not let a smile erupt.

"Neha, he loves you."

She looked at my lips, perhaps seeing my emphasis on 'loves'.

"Right?"

She seemed to nod. An answer is an answer. I had to take it.

"Gizzy has gone to sleep," I said.

She peered down, to peep into the dead eyes of the bear.

"So, you go to sleep now. Okay?"

"Okay," she mumbled, and turned to her right and hid her head inside her folded arms, gently crashing into the pillow.

I switched off the lamp. There was nothing bright anymore... all the gold and the yellow hues that lit her toys, her small pink cushions, her face, and the brownish dots inside her eyes, had turned grey. There she slept, in her own dark space, stifling all her questions. I gently got up, and patted down the blanket covering her. I picked up the faintly ticking table clock and took it with me. I did not want to leave any sound unattended in the room, which could wake her up. I slowly closed the door, stepped out and took a deep breath.

I clenched the railing of the staircase and climbed down the stairs with heavy, laboured steps. I thought, with each step, some answers that I knew, but many more that I craved. In the dimly lit living room, I centred my eyes on the fridge. I opened it and pulled out a bottle of cold water and banged it on the dining table. I took out a chair and settled myself. I didn't rest, I didn't slouch. I sat firm, straight and looked up the climbing flight of stairs. I wondered if she had slept. I swiftly opened the lid of the bottle and took a heavy gulp. My mouth gaped to breathe hard, letting off a fragmented puff of air. My eyes left roving for a while, caught hold of our marriage photo, framed on the wall opposite the fridge. I smiled at it. I wanted to let off a burst of laughter. But I saw my phone lying on the other edge of the table.

I hunched to grab it, unlocked it, and tapped the button with the green symbol on the bottom panel. I saw the first name in my call-log. I wavered my index finger closer, playing over it. I thought to tap on it, but did not. I stared at that name for a whole one minute. And then I called *him*.

"Hello." He picked up after four anxious rings. He sounded like he was woken up, alarmed, disturbed.

"Where are you?" I asked.

"Where else?"

I didn't answer. I rested my back on the chair and didn't take my eyes off the staircase. I wanted to ignore the questions popping up in my head that gave a sense of hope: *Why did he answer my call? Why did he care to talk? Why did he make time? Why would he do that?*

"Ashima?" he cut through my thoughts, "What happened?"

I said nothing to that voice. I held myself, so he could think, a bit more...

I had met him, Alok, in a library, when I least expected to meet anyone. Two months back... it was one of those

Saturday afternoons when I felt angry and restless at home and wanted to lock myself somewhere and read. It was one of those days when I managed Neha to get to sleep and leave her under nanny's care, even if for an hour. When I could step out and breathe... One of those weekends when Rahul, my husband, spent more precious time with his friend, his new-found love.

Rahul would visit her and they would switch off their phones and disappear for hours together. He would return home by two or three the next morning, but after cleverly calling me in the evening to speak to Neha and create normalcy. The normalcy of two happy parents being there for their five-year-old daughter, who had reached the cusp of sensing the meaning of unspoken things. Things. Like the thick air of silence between us when we had our short, quick dinners. The long dragging absences when Daddy simply won't come home after office, and called us at fixed times. The loud fights she could barely hear, after we had to shut doors and order her nanny to take her out of the house. But I never suffered a bruise. Rahul ensured that. Just as he ensured that I never fell short of domestic needs. He showed all signs of disinterest and disconnect and, although he never said it, a need to divorce me on the grounds of incompatibility leaving no obvious traces of abuse or suffering, except for our occasional loud fights, where I became the louder, angrier one. Infidelity was no longer a crime, but a reason for divorce, but here... it wasn't just about that. He knew how to leverage his financial situation, that he earned so much more than I did before we had Neha, and he could support Neha by all means. He knew I struggled to get a job, that I was on a much-extended post-maternity break, and all I wanted was to be close to my daughter. He seamlessly transitioned from a doting husband in our initial months of marriage, to an angry, unsatisfied one – and one fine day, he converted to an ardent lover of someone else, much younger, and I guess prettier. But he never dropped the father's hat to keep in touch with Neha. He addressed her needs, including her frustrating questions like 'Why aren't you home yet?'

He almost behaved like a single, caring father. Could he have equal rights to visit his daughter, if we divorced? Who could be sure? He created the environment, over the last one year, which was enough for him to have Neha, after our official separation that he meticulously planned in his head. A year that rushed ahead of me, to close in… on my sudden meeting with Alok.

"It's past one o'clock. Tell me? Hello?" Alok was now fully awake.

The time didn't bother me. It didn't feel like it bothered him.

"Let me step outside," he said. He lived with his mother, who wasn't aware about us, yet.

"You didn't call, earlier today," I said.

"I tried in the evening. It didn't connect. Then I got stuck."

"Where?"

"Why are you asking?"

"Because I want to."

"Just the routine things, Ashima. There's nothing that I don't tell you."

"I should not have waited for your call."

"Why did you wait?"

"Because I am used to..." I sensed my voice rising. "You know - I am used to waiting for calls. Then, arguing over messages. And then I get a message from him. You know, like a signal. A closure. An explanation that I must buy at face-value. As if it's my duty—"

"Listen. You calm down." He tried to diffuse an outburst, as he often did when I vented out.

Who was he? Did I know him well? When we met in the library, it was a simple, unremarkable chat. I pushed through the glass door and expected our regular librarian, Mr. Mohanty, the bespectacled, round elderly face with thick brown-framed glasses and an everlasting grin stuck under a bushy moustache. But *he* surprised me. A charming handsome man, probably in the mid-30s, with a light, neatly set beard, hair side-parted, a chiselled jawline, and a smile that slowly crept open to reveal the twinkle in his deep black eyes. He explained why Mr. Mohanty had to resign, but that sounded so irrelevant when I grabbed a moment to stare into his eyes. He carried the polite professional tone when he asked about my membership details, and the agility of a teenager, when he searched the shelves for an old forgotten book that I deliberately requested, thinking he wouldn't find it, so I could get more time to look at him, as he walked around the shelves, bending, standing and crouching to fetch a copy. How else could I have noticed him, if I hadn't lied about a book I supposedly wanted to read! Taking a seat close to his desk or stealing glances while reading a book would have been too obvious, in a place as quiet and yet as watchful as a reading room stuffed with young smart students. He came back with a low, sullen face that looked cuter and apologized for not having the book, but assured that he will get a copy next time. I seized the chance to explain a bit more, by lying about how much I liked it. I settled for another book on that day. And in the days that followed, I could settle for any book that he found or recommended. It wasn't long before he found the signs in my demeanour that he asked me how I was doing in my life. And my hesitant answers met with more of his curious questions, till I unlocked the details of my home...

Yes, we went out. Gradually. We met for coffee. We couldn't spend long hours as I had to be back home. At least *one* parent had to be back home. We met at cafes, a bit away from my home, so no one could spot us. No one in my vicinity. He got an able assistant who could replace him for an hour or so in the library, overlapping his lunchtime, and he met me. My visits to the library stopped, but my husband presumed that I was there, while he got busy in his work and found time to exchange messages and emojis with his girlfriend. There was no way any student would have found out, and imagine that the librarian went out to meet an old customer. And, thus we went out. We talked. Briefly. Intensely. Being as open as we could. Judging as little as possible. For an hour or less. Every day or every alternate day. Over the last month or so. We talked till we parted. Initially, we found our time too short and childishly expressed that we would look forward to our next chat. Then we saw the value of speaking face-to-face, in a city that hardly spoke. We cherished our little time. Our conversations grew deeper. We set them free. And returning home felt less shackling. We shared nothing more. An accidental touch of fingers, or a wrist held while crossing the road, or an arm around the shoulder, rather barely above it, scraping the thin air. But we didn't hold hands. We didn't hug. We hadn't so far. Though we both wanted it. So badly.

I could rely on him. Simply to talk and create a little life out of it. Though I didn't know where this was headed. But I knew I wasn't a stepping stone for him. That he had not come out of a break-up, or such baggage, only to meet me and find comfort. He was simply a case of someone, who had been all by himself for quite some time, waiting for the person on whom he could pin his serious hopes. I guess that's why he measured his words so often.

"Ashima, are you there?" he woke me up from my trance.

"Yes... sorry, I kept thinking —" I stopped for a bit to ask him a question he was familiar with. "My daughter is five years old. What do I tell her?"

"She is five, so you *can* tell her, something. It's better than when she grows older. Isn't it?"

"So, I should lie to her, about her father's affair, till she is older?"

"You don't agree?" he said. "Ashima, look for what you can do. There is enough already that you cannot."

"Why don't you be in my place and then you would know."

"I am trying to put myself there."

"You can't."

"I said I am trying."

Yes, he was. He heard me, when I judged his abilities.

Alok paused for a while and asked, "What did Rahul say?"

"He said he won't come home tonight. That I should tell Neha that Daddy is working overtime and sleeping in the office. I told him, I cannot lie to her. We argued a bit and I hung up the phone. And, he didn't call back."

Alok went mum for some time.

Did he have an option? They say, staying quiet is often the most sensible thing to do. I say, it's an easy thing (and not calling someone back is way easier). Yes, I judged Alok. Whatever we had... hadn't set itself so strong that I could begin to trust. To trust someone was hard, given my own situation. I didn't feel so alone, though, because of him. Because he could pick up my call, even at this time of the night. Though it was only two months back I had met him the first time, but something made me think that what we shared was not frivolous.

"Ashima. You are not alone," he blurted out.

"I guess."

"No, that's what you feel right now. There. In your home without anyone. At this odd time. That's what you feel."

"Okay."

"Really, you are not alone."

"If you say so."

"Don't do that."

"Do what."

"Am I making this any easier for you?"

"I am not sure."

"You are not sure?" his voice changed.

I didn't answer. I was not thinking clearly. I pursed my lips. *Why* did I say that?

"Ashima, just tell me..." he cut himself for a second, and went on: "Do I have a place, in your scheme of things? Any place?"

"I meant..." I stopped, to hold back an immediate flurry of words. "I don't know where we both are headed. You know how people think. I am married. You are a friend. A friend of a married woman. A new, male friend. That doesn't sound good, does it? It's disgusting. Isn't it?"

"Why do you have to frame it like *they* do?"

"Then how should I say it?"

"Ask yourself."

"I called you because I just wanted to talk to you," I said.

"Not really. We have been talking about each other for some time now."

"I have never denied that we are friends," I said.

"Please ask yourself. A clear question by all means. Do I have a place in your scheme of things?"

"Am I cheating anyone? Is talking to you at this time, wrong?"

"Not those. Those are pointless questions."

"Why don't you tell me since you know it?" I almost shouted, only to realize that Neha was asleep upstairs.

"Why did you pick up the phone?" he said. "Ask *that*. Why did you call someone at this time? When you had to lie to your child? Ask *that*. When you got disgusted at the thought of checking where your husband is. When things fell apart, why did you pick up the phone? Why did you call someone else? And why did I answer your call? Ask *that*."

I didn't speak. I heard forceful breathing on the other side that surged and collapsed.

"I am sorry," he said. "Ashima? Just ignore that, please…" I pictured him, pleading into the phone, trying to figure out my quietness.

"I am being selfish. I know."

I didn't answer.

"Ashima? You there?"

I shut my eyes. He said these things that shut me up. Things that were not just curious suggestions or wise remarks. He said things forcefully. He meant them. He wanted to say things, to focus on what lay ahead of us. He wanted to steal the thoughts that rattled my head… thoughts of my marriage, my home, my daughter. He single-mindedly wanted to deflect me from my turmoil, which in the initial days, looked like an immature act. But, it took me weeks to realize that his attempts to buffer me were the reasons that made me call him. So, I asked myself. Why did I call him? Well, some people reduce it to the term 'friendship', an easy way to describe it.

I realized I had taken a long pause. I asked him:

"What do you want to know, Alok?"

"That, what am I? Am I a sounding board?" he asked.

"No."

"A punching bag?"

"No."

"A trouble-shooter?"

"No."

"A patient ear?"

"No."

"A friend?"

I didn't answer.

"A friend?" he asked vigorously.

"I think so," I said.

"After two months, you say *that*." He smothered a mocking giggle and said, "I am sorry, but glad rather, that you accept me as that."

We didn't talk for a while. I looked fleetingly at the foot of the staircase, almost as if he managed to drive my mind off, from the bedroom and from Neha, even for some time. At least I didn't look at the marriage photo. At least, I drifted a little. Into his conversation. At least I argued with him.

I said something to break the stillness:

"Things are straight here. Rahul loves his daughter, perhaps the only bit of our marriage that he loves. He wants her and will have her." I paused, to shoulder the weight of my words. "No one can stop him. To people who don't know us, they both would appear like an inseparable father and daughter. They do, even today when he gets time to take her out."

"Ashima, wait—" he interrupted, "Don't speak as if she is not your daughter."

"I would never get custody."

"I am not talking about that," he said. "I am saying you must tell her soon. Even tomorrow. When you both are alone. You have to explain to her, the whole situation."

"She is five. Do you think she has the capacity to understand this?"

"Do you have the capacity to bear all of this, till she grows older by a year or two to understand it? How much more would you lie to her?"

"I don't know—"

"Wait," he said, "And what about her? What will she think – about you lying to her, when she is older? About her father lying to her? She needs to be set free as much as you need to."

"You are effectively telling me to file for a divorce, first," I said.

"It will happen anyway, whoever files first. I am saying – Neha should be set free, so, you should tell her your reason to separate from Rahul. This is a matter of time. Let her see for herself what's happening. And her father's supposed concern for his family. Let her observe. When you initiate this separation, it will be at least a year till you see any result. Let her go through it… you help her take it steadily and in her own way—"

"No—"

"She has a right to that too."

"I don't have the courage to confront Rahul and do this to Neha."

"Really? Doesn't look like that to me. You asked me, some time back, if you should lie to her till she grows older, didn't you? Surely, you don't like that option. Surely, you want the situation to move ahead and not remain hanging. You are not waiting for him to end this long-dragged torture and take a decision, are you? If he is unapologetic, so should you be."

I held back, a low smile. It was strange. Why the smile?

My smile would show in my voice. I clenched it hard. I didn't want him to know that.

> He calmed down. But the air felt curious. Impatient.
>
> He asked me, what he had to:
>
> "What about the married woman's *new male friend*?"
>
> "I don't know where he's going. Why can't he see the uncertainty that I see?"
>
> "Because he feels certain when she calls him."
>
> "Does he?"
>
> "Yes."
>
> "Does he know there is a strength… that I gather?"
>
> "From?"
>
> "Yeah… It is strange. I hear you and I want to say things—"
>
> "Things?"
>
> "Things, that I can't say."
>
> "To whom?"
>
> "To myself. And at home."
>
> "You don't say them to me either," he said.
>
> I hid a smile, again.
>
> "Do you?" he asked.
>
> "I expect less."
>
> "So?"
>
> "So, I don't end up speaking those things to you."
>
> "But you keep thinking them."
>
> "Sort of."

"What are you thinking?" he asked me.

"That, no hearts are racing. No castles in the air. No wishful thoughts. No song and dance. Nothing to hold on to. No images that make me curious. No pining to hear someone's voice…"

"And?"

"And yet, something feels familiar. As if I know it so well, by now. Else, I won't call you. I feel I am talking to someone who's… who's right here. With me. Across this table. In my home."

"Why didn't you say that before?" he asked.

"You just want everything to be said?"

"I can't help it."

"And then you want it to be clarified."

"No."

"And then you want it to be repeated, to confirm."

"Okay. Stop it!" he said. Maybe, he smiled, this time.

"Alok," I said, "I just want to trust someone. The whole world may say it's a big word. But, I feel it's basic. The most minimum. But, it sounds hopeless—"

"Can you trust me?" he butted in, "Can you trust me that I would walk with you, on the rocky road that lies ahead? Through your conflict with Rahul and your adjustment with Neha. Do you think I will stand by you?"

I didn't want to hurt him. I wish I could dodge and deflect his question, as well as he helped me deflect my rattling thoughts. I wish I could take him away from his thoughts or just hug him.

"Why do you want to know, now?" I asked.

"Just tell me, can you trust me?"

"It's not an easy answer—"

"Tell me."

I didn't answer.

"Please tell me."

"Do you have a complete idea of what you are asking?"

"Tell me."

I refused to speak, which made him wait, and wait all the more.

Alok knew that my life would not change tomorrow. That seeing my husband's face in the morning would trigger inside me, all kinds of aggressive emotions that I will suppress. He knew that, what *we* shared was often inexplicable to us. It had inherent doubts and questions, due to its newness and uncertainties. It had no sanction from the society we lived in. It was fragile, maybe a bit strange. Yet, it screamed for space. But, he did give me, a person, someone to look forward to. That I had someone to talk to. That I had someone to better understand. And he made me think that I have another small life that I could build, brick by brick, within a large daunting suffocating one. He made me think that I could normalize, with slow, hesitant steps.

I had taken a long while. He still waited. I said:

"I don't know about trust. But I can listen to you. I don't want to hurt you when you stay by my side."

"Then meet me tomorrow, for breakfast."

"What?" I heard myself chuckle.

"You heard me."

"Are you serious?"

"What do you think?"

"Look—"

"No. You look! You don't have to... well... listen - you don't have to face Rahul first thing in the morning. Just make some time, take a cab and meet me at *our* café. Message him that you are meeting a friend and will be back in an hour. Can you do that? Can we do this, please?"

I thought through, but couldn't take much time.

"Okay."

He got still for a second. I heard him breathe out, then I heard nothing. Maybe it rested him, a little. Perhaps, he let a thought fly away... or grasped an ounce of hope. Perhaps, he smiled.

I sensed it all and I could only let him, be.

# Deaf

It was a big day for my sister, yet she was losing hope. I was speaking to her since the day before.

"You have no idea how this feels," she said.

"You are right, I can never know," I said. "But you are in charge."

Priti kept mum. She sniffed, maybe she was wiping her tears.

"You heard me? You are in charge of your situation."

"How?" she yelled.

"Calm down. Please. Okay – let's do it this way. You listen to the nurses, and no one else. Ask them questions. Don't get distracted by your in-laws. You will get a lot of advice. But just focus on what the nurse tells you. Can you do that for me?"

"Sourabh is reaching in an hour. But it will be late, I know."

"Isn't it enough that he is desperately trying to be

there? And, why your husband's absence should be the most important thing, right now?"

"Because I don't want anyone else but him."

"You have your baby waiting to come out. Please think about that, just that."

"Prachi, I don't have the strength."

"No one has, in such times. But listen to the doctor, the nurses. They are around you. For them, this is a routine. So trust them, will you?"

She didn't answer, but I thought she heard me fully.

Deepak had arrived by 4 pm... but I was already on the call. He took off his jacket and his sweater and hinted that he needed an immediate shower. I nodded. He looked exhausted with a curious frown on his face that refused to disappear. He had a two-week winter break but wanted to come to Boston just for four days to spend time with me. This was odd, but I didn't think much. It was all too fast: he called me last night, he had already booked his train, he informed me about his stay and he hung up... as he was busy sending some course submissions, which he had delayed. We were together for almost two years, but the distance never mattered – we made good use of our semester breaks, our weekends with the four-hour travel between us, and lots of video calls. In fact, the distance brought with it, a natural space that we didn't need to create. So, his call, last night, was a bit quick. Yet, I chucked the questions that popped in my head. I thought I will make him stay longer. I too, was in the thick of my Master's, with the average results of my previous semester exam looming over my mind, and Priti's situation... far away in India.

"I will hang up now," she said.

"Wait —"

"Prachi, I need to hang up. They are going to try again and induce labour. This is all getting crazy. Like I am a device that will be restarted."

"Okay, okay - you will remember what I said?"

"Those are just words."

"I know. But do they make sense? Just, please, if you could keep them in mind."

"I will try —"

"Everything that we have been speaking since yesterday. You will remember?"

"Forcibly?"

"Yes. Forcibly."

"Okay," she sighed.

"It's only about you now, and your child. It will be over before you know."

"Yeah," she paused for a moment and hung up.

Deepak stepped out of the shower and went straight to the bedroom, locked, changed, and stepped out to go to the kitchen to make coffee. I stared at my phone, imagining what could happen with Priti. And her loneliness, and the burden of a child, which they both never wanted at the stage they were in, but got to terms with it. And, yet, Deepak's silence and a strange kind of aloofness started to distract me. After we exchanged our smiles and hugs, I told him what was happening with my sister. He nodded, heard intently, and said that she will be fine. He repeated that twice – that, she will be fine. That's about it. He didn't build onto that topic.

..................................

About an hour later, I found myself on a train. Hordes of people climbed onto the bogie and crowded by the minute. All I could see were men and women, their chins down, immersed in their phones or staring at their shoes, holding their bags close, clutching the overhead steel-grey bars. There were also a few college students, whispering to each other, joking and giggling among themselves, some even dozing off on nearby shoulders. The train made violent jolts in between, on the left and the right, in its meandering course like a hurried aimless toddler. A feature of the Green Line.

I didn't have a bag to hug, nor an arm to lean upon. The wall was too stiff to rest my head on. Deepak faced the door. He checked his phone and got busy with messaging. I could see him, catch fleeting views of his head amongst many others. I lost sight of it, every few seconds, as the heads in between swayed with the movement of the train. Before the crowds flowed in, he went ahead to stand near the door. He let me sit. All by myself. I curled a little, to huddle against the wall and let my gaze fix on an adjacent tall man's carbon-black overcoat. All my thoughts that had been racing hard for the past one hour came to a screeching halt. All I could see was the deepening blackness of his overcoat. Now, I could only hear voices, barely audible, broken and scattered. Deepak's voice, or the voices of our conversations that we had just yesterday, or the day before. I wished more people had entered the bogie. To fill the palpable distance between us. To fill in the gaps left between my shoes and his, my knees and his, and the shiny steel spaces between my fists holding the vertical steel-grey bars, and his. I wished more people would come to fill in all the possible cracks, so I could feel their hands and knees and shoes touching mine. He didn't come in, he wanted to be at the door all by himself. Think of his ways ahead. And to make him sit, so I could sit on his lap in a crowded train, was an option discarded.

We ate pretzels and threw the tissues in the bin, just before we took the train. While sugar cubes stuck on our lips, the bin was left to stink. Abandoned. The brown crunchy pretzel was his suggestion, or a distraction. A distraction to indulge me. To get me inside a dark harrowing cave without a guiding torch. To prime me for a major change. To prepare me to understand. Understand the words that he had uttered, at my home, an hour ago. Words that sparked hot blistering bulbs in my head. Words that sounded casual but meant harsh things. Words that hit me and left me puzzled. Words that inflamed a nerve in my head. A nagging, begging, clinging, unconvinced nerve. Words that shocked. Rattled. Confused. Someone inside me began to throw a volley of questions. One by one, all the nuts and bolts of control I had over myself began to slip away, like mice that fled before an earthquake or a flood. And a strange hibernating creature inside my body woke up and began to shout. Louder and Louder. Posing questions that ridiculed me. Questions tumbling out like coins saved for months together, out of a piggy bank's broken back: 'What do you mean?' 'Why won't this work?' 'Are you joking?' 'Why are you bringing this up? 'Why are you joking?' 'Why do you look at me like that?' 'Why don't you look at me?' 'Tell me?'

"I am not ready, Prachi." He had said that, at home, after we had settled in... sat on the floor against a wall, my head rested on his shoulders. I straightened to look at him, almost ignoring what I heard and wanted him to say it again. He refused to make eye-contact.

"Don't say it won't work," I said.

"I don't want it to."

"Please."

"Are you listening? I am not ready."

"I heard it."

"Nor will I ever be ready."

"For?"

"For all that you want!"

"Which is?"

"You know well."

I didn't answer.

"For things ahead. A relationship? Remember? Something serious?"

"Yes."

"It makes me uncomfortable. I don't want that. It freaks me out."

"It can't be so bad."

"It's too fast. Something way ahead of dating. Something I haven't given a thought to, ever. And you knew that." he said.

"We don't have to go fast."

"Yes, we don't!"

"It's been two years…only… We…we don't have to hurry things."

"No, you do. You're saying this to calm me down. We both know that you have to."

"No, there is no such thing," I said.

"Don't lie. Don't avoid this topic. Face it."

"Please don't get worked up…"

"It worries me. And then I can't breathe in this relationship, if - if I can even call it *that*."

"Please."

"Listen. The more I think about it, about you, the more it makes me…"

"What?"

"You know me. You knew what you were getting into. You knew, right?"

"What does it make you?"

"We are frank enough. You know what I don't want."

"Makes you?"

"That's not important."

"Makes you?"

"It makes me like you less," Deepak said that and shut himself for a minute. He let off a deep breath. "You heard it?"

"How?"

"I don't know. I don't want to be near this."

"Near me?"

"Stop asking. It's you who's getting worked up. It's not about you."

"Who else?" I faked a smile.

He looked at me… and then to the wall facing us. "Prachi, this is about what you want and how that cannot work."

"What's so wrong? It can't be so bad."

"See. This is where we go. All the rights and the wrongs that I should clarify." He shook his head in frustration.

"You clarify for me?"

He didn't answer.

"What is it that you want?" I asked.

"I want to leave tomorrow. I want to go back to New York."

"You have come here for a break. For us."

"And I will cancel it. Will reschedule my train, to tomorrow. I came to tell you, all the way... yes, so that I don't have to tell you over the phone."

I took some time to let that sentence pass through me.

"Is there someone else?" I asked.

"No."

"Are you sure?"

"Please."

"It's not Mohita right?"

"Are you seriously bringing her up?" He looked straight into my eyes and spoke in a rough tone, which I ... didn't understand.

"Well, we fought about it, due to her, a week ago," I continued, "We might as well talk about her again."

"Is it not enough that we have brought her up, few times before?" he raised his voice for the first time in the conversation. "Each time I had to clarify, the Whys and the Hows? Seriously, it's not enough for you?"

"Then, just tell me what's going on."

He didn't answer. He breathed hard and kept staring at his shoes parked against the door.

"Are you sure that all this, is just about you not wanting to commit?" I asked.

"Wait - to commit is a big big thing for me. And, I have brought this up earlier, but you avoided the topic."

"Because I thought it will change with time. You will change with time. You will stop getting anxious about it."

"It should come from within! The feeling to commit. It can't be an effort, a step that I have to learn to cross. Do you get it?"

"Okay—"

"No, wait. The point is - you are not letting me be myself, in this whole dragged equation of ours. Honestly, I can't take it ahead and I must move on."

A lot had happened after he said that. I asked more questions. He gave more answers. The quiet, aloof, frowning person who came to my home, when I was busy on a call with Priti, had become vocal, loud, precise and defensive. We fought. I shouted. He shouted back. My eyes welled... his didn't. After loud voices and pointless convincing, more on my part, we both thought that we could go out. We didn't need to talk. We just needed fresh air. And, what better than going to the Observatory to see the decorations. It was the evening of the 25th of December.

Another jolt, and the train came to a stop at the next station, and so did the little world I made in my head. I couldn't scream, so I tried to centre my eyes and my energies. To move away from the faces around me, the smiles, the whispers, my chaotic thoughts and a hundred questions colliding with recent memories, hugs and laughter. People began to step out. The man with the deep black overcoat on which I had fixed my eyes, had vanished. Black was hard to be found. A black that was pure and honest. The complete absence of light. The colour that sucked in all light, unapologetically. The absence of colour. The absence that lured me in. The void I wanted to creep in, to hide myself.

But the world didn't let me hide. People began to move ahead. I was forced to get up. Move slowly. No sliding shoulders. No jostling. No yelling. I watched his head gently slip down as he got down from the train. I kept my eyes on the grey floor imprinted with dusty brown shoe scuffs, clutched the vertical steel-grey stands, and stepped out.

Deepak stood there, waiting. Waiting? I saw a total absence of emotion on his face. Who was this man looking at me, as if to check? To check, whether I was moving... moving ahead.

We walked, leaving a few steps between us. He walked ahead. I followed. We stepped out of the subway. A tall building with shining yellow windows towered over our heads. We entered the Observatory, a skyscraper offering a view of the entire city. I refused to take the elevator to the top floor. That put him off, but he held his reaction back. Instead, he suggested we walk around to see the Christmas decorations. Was that another distraction? Like a pretzel? Was the decor now supposed to grab my attention... was it to act like a bar of chocolate to munch on?

The place was made to look studded. Multiple shrubs of mistletoe leaves, beaded with golden lights, were placed on either side – the leaves were wrapped together, stripped off their natural selves. A few large golden gleaming baubles dangled from the ceiling on invisible strings, like static planets in different orbits dutifully encircling a silver shining star fixed at the apex of a tall lush green Christmas tree, with fake snowflakes piled on its thin tender branches, amidst the ruby-red, golden-yellow and rose-pink baubles that stuck to its leaves. The baubles acted like moons, beaming in the ambient light with no spark of their own. The tree was an assortment. A prepared mass of green, gold, white and red. A source of beauty to grab eyeballs. Eyeballs that would stare in wonder and take photos. Till it suited them. Till they moved on to other decorations.

A snow-laden shack with white roofs and windows without panes caught my eyes. The chimney was white, as were the shrubs on the lawn. The white blades of grass had artificial snowflakes dumped on them. The chimney had no smoke to emit. Because the house had no faces inside. The gate had no post-box. No foot-prints. It was not anyone's house. It was an arrangement. A place to shelter an old man in a grotesque red attire. Tired already from his long, arduous journey from the Arctic, carrying numerous heavy bags stuffed with a zillion gifts for the kids who peeked into the house. Snow-covered reindeer statues were parked on the lawn. They knelt in the grass, silent, thoughtful, staring into space...

Deepak was unaffected. He walked straight, with an air of certainty, even though his still, expressionless face refused to change. His phone kept him busy, he would pull it out of his pocket, answer messages and tuck it back in. He did that quite often, sometimes hurriedly, sometimes slowly, as if to answer each and every message. At times, he typed with both hands, to focus. Once, in the middle of the typing, he turned to me and seemed to think harder about something. A furrow appeared on his brow... and after a while, he let it go - the thought that bugged him. He distracted himself with the decorations. He seemed to be someone... who suddenly wanted to explore. Look for beauty. Look for calm. He showed an interest in the place as if he wanted to look for energy in the lights and sounds, and the children shouting and running around, and the rich red attire of the famous old man that we know, and his funny black belt, and the shining planets above our heads. Energy to keep him going. He was a free man.

We walked side by side, but kept enough distance between us, so that someone could pass through it, assuming we weren't together. We weren't. A kid could run a reindeer sleigh right between us.

I began to go deaf. The more carols I heard, the heavier my throat felt. The lyrics lost their structure to become shapeless masses of sound and they disappeared in their loops of meaning. Tunes lost their form. The songs seemed like high-pitched incessantly rising and falling waves. Noise, which I could not connect with. I lost touch with each and every character, each and every being that studded this place. Its sights, sounds, colours, faces, pace, and music. Everything was meaningless because of what he had said, a little more than an hour ago. How could I understand? How could I not see it coming?

A row of marble benches lined some fountains ahead of us. The fountains were straight short spurts of clear water, making small whorls in the air, then falling back without a sound. We sat there, maintaining our distance and stared at the people walking around us. He fixed his gaze on the Christmas tree, as though its bright lights and colours would shield him from me.

My eyes refused to look at them any differently than earlier. They were not a thing of beauty, not a joy for even a moment. They made me go into a deep spell of thought, where I heard my unanswered questions.

Finally, he broke the silence: "Can I say something?"

I didn't answer. I kept staring at the water whorls.

He carried on, "I know you won't take this in a wrong way. Because you know what I think about you. And I am a bit afraid to utter the word, love".

I looked at him. I felt like a curious child waiting for the next thing he would say.

"Please don't ever think that I have stopped loving you. I can't. You are such a dear friend. I love you. I love you. I love you. Not the way you do. But I can go on saying that. That I love you. Because I really do. And I don't want to stop myself from saying that to my friend—"

"You have a friend here, right?" I stopped his train of thought.

"What?"

"A friend? Yours?"

"Here?"

I paused to take a breath. "Doesn't he live two stations away? The doctor? We were going tomorrow to his place for dinner? I mean, we had planned it."

"Yes. Why?"

"Stay at his place tonight. Come tomorrow to my apartment to take your bags." I stood up.

"What? Wait..." He didn't get up. "Prachi?"

He fidgeted in his seat. Was he surprised? Was he keen

to let me stay? I didn't know. My last bits of expectation tried to shake my firmness. I said:

"You want to return tomorrow? Then reschedule your train now. I have to go home."

I turned my back on him and started walking towards the revolving glass door behind the fountains. He didn't call my name. In a strange impulse, I turned back and blurted it out –

"Go on, message... and finish the chat that's keeping you busy. With whoever it is."

...................................

I exited the building and called a cab. I reached the T-station. The underground Red Line awaited me. The train that rarely took strange turns. Never jerked and jolted. It ran a straight, self-assured and fast course on a sturdy, linear track.

As I entered the train, Priti flashed in my head. But I couldn't make myself call her. I didn't want to call anyone. What would have happened to her? I told myself to call her after reaching home and not delay that.

This train was empty. Perhaps the whole world was partying. Heading home at seven in the evening on Christmas was odd. The emptiness made the vertical steel bars look shinier. They seemed to be more in number than on the last train. Grey seats with white borders separated the bars. Why were some of the seats arranged in pairs? What had the makers assumed? The grey floor had old, white streaks on it, from years and years of scuffing footsteps. The tube-lights above me joined hands and glittered. Glittered for the sake of duty. The windows were deep black rectangles that reflected the seats and the half-a-dozen lifeless posters stuck on the walls. Posters of ads, with bright smiling faces that assured happiness of some kind or other. The few pivoted handles, above on the horizontal steel bars, seemed inhibited. The pace of an unoccupied train sapped their energies.

Till the train stopped, someone entered and pulled one of them.

"Do you have a dollar, Ma'am?" He was a white man dressed in a tattered grey shirt, an old brown jacket and grey trousers, with long golden hair and yellow teeth, one of them partially broken in the centre. He was barefoot.

"No," I said.

"You must have something."

"I don't have a dollar. I have a twenty."

He smiled.

"I am sorry."

"You know, I feel like going out today."

"You do?"

"It's beautiful out there. Isn't it?"

"It is."

"It's so cold. I… look at me and my jacket. I will die if I step out."

"No, you won't."

"I will fall ill."

"Maybe."

"If I eat a sandwich, I may not."

"Hmm…"

"I could then step out, for a while."

"Yes."

"It's biting cold. Freezing."

"Yeah."

"I have nothing. This day. This evening."

I looked at him, into the sinking brown eyes. I couldn't decide whether it was innocence I saw there, or something else.

"I want to eat," he repeated.

He didn't twitch a muscle. He didn't flinch. He didn't breathe. He only kept staring at me. It didn't scare me. Strangely, I didn't feel uncomfortable.

"I don't have a dollar. If I give you twenty, I will have to walk home."

"I have nothing. You have twenty."

"I will have to walk."

"I walk all day. I have nothing."

"I too have nothing, Sir."

"You do." He smiled.

"You know nothing."

"I know you do."

"Nothing at all. Not what you think."

He smiled again and said, "You have a home."

I gazed at his smile. His wide, beaming, yellow-toothed smile. There was nothing more to be said or asked. I opened my bag and handed him the note. He got down at the next station.

……………………………

I turned the knob of my main door and let myself in. The eerie silence of the living room heard the creaking of the door, and like tentacles, it crawled onto my skin. I closed the door, bolted it and rested my back against it. I looked into the darkness that engulfed the tall windows, spilling over onto the carpet and casting its black shadows on the beige roughness of the flat, dead carpet. The room was dimly lit. Traces of yellow light spilled from the kitchen. The air was still and bereft. There was nothing that it could claim as its own. No smells of a closed room shared with another person. No suppressed sounds. No sense of belonging or living. It tried to scream that a person lived here. Laughed here, slept here, hugged here, or used to… so often… just last weekend. That is the wall where we had kissed, a bit clunkily. Where I had felt, for the first time, that something was odd. Or maybe I had denied that oddity for days before. Refused to acknowledge it for weeks before. There was a kiss. But a reciprocation that seemed… polite or necessary. Why did he not avoid that?

That was the spot on the carpet where we had dinner last weekend. A dinner that saw more of my questions and less of his answers. My anecdotes and smiles, and his nodding. A chatterbox himself, nodding and listening to me? Why hadn't I read more into it? There, next to the shoe rack… his bags were parked when he came home earlier today, the bags which were now sleeping in the bedroom. Every element of this room spoke of my times spent with Deepak. He had broken it all and left me. Not literally, yet. But in the way that mattered. The Whys and the Hows were my companions now, dissecting what had happened. Knowing myself and knowing my inner voices, I knew that this was not something that time could dissolve.

The cordless phone rang all of a sudden, sending shock-waves into the air from the coffee-table that hit my ears. I resisted moving and kept hearing the mechanical rings. I let four rings pass, unattended. Then, I rushed to pick up on the fifth. It was my mother:

"Hello? Prachi?"

I didn't answer.

"Hello?... Hello? Prachi?"

"Yeah. Sorry, I was sleeping."

"Oh. But how? I thought Deepak had come. He came today, right?"

"Yes."

"Didn't you both go out?"

"What happened Mom, tell me?"

"You should have been here."

"Why?"

"They are all talking about you, Priti, Sourabh and her in-laws." I sensed that she smiled, and thought that she could have hugged me... had I been there.

"Oh, Priti delivered?"

"Yesss... And it's a beautiful girl. She's been trying to call you for two hours, but your phone..."

"Phone?" My fingers scrambled down the narrow front pocket of my jeans to pull out the silenced phone. I clicked the home button and saw twenty missed calls.

"I am so sorry... my God... but why was she calling?"

"What has happened to you? We all know that you both spoke earlier today and have been speaking since yesterday."

"Yeah, but..."

"No, you did."

"Well..."

"She is thrilled. She is crying. She didn't realize she could deliver. Without an operation. All by herself, with that enormous pain... more in her case. But she did!"

"Yeah."

"We had lost hope. We all agreed for surgery. You know that."

"Yes." I felt a strange weight in my throat. "There was no need," I said. "She shouldn't have called. She should rest."

"The doctors said she was too tired. But we could try once more. That's when she spoke to you. And it all changed."

"No, no... you are just being..."

"Being what?"

"Mom, I just tried. I couldn't do much being several time-zones away."

"It's never about the distance."

"No..." I strangely wanted her to stop.

"You guided her. Made her feel that you were there, bearing it with her, giving her the time she needed."

"It's okay..." I wanted her to stop it right there. All of it.

"Don't you realize what you did?"

"I am not a doctor. I just spoke to her."

"Prachi, this is not just about delivering a child."

"Then what is it?"

"She was in pain. She felt lonely. Sourabh came much later, an hour after we saw the baby. She was uneasy, even with us. She screamed even when she was exhausted. She missed you. Every minute."

"I didn't realize I would—"

"You were kind. Strong. She took it from you. At the right time. To do what she wanted to. And that goes beyond distances..."

"Mom... Listen..." I thought my voice broke.

"Okay, I will stop. Fine. And now you call her, after some time. Okay?"

"Okay." I didn't want to cut the call. But I feared she would sense that something was wrong at my end.

But she said what she had to. And she hung up.

I kept the phone on the table. I moved to the blinds. I dropped my cell-phone. It fell on the carpet with a mild thud. The blinds were firmly closed. Not a movement, not a breath. Gentle, fickle, long edges held each other, their dusty fingers joined in. I let my fingers run through the length of the blinds. I nestled my face against them, rattled them a little. I tried to hear a familiar sound. I pressed my ears to the blinds to catch a voice, now gone. I closed my eyes to grab a memory, destroyed. I craved an image, invisible. I craved an ounce of strength, some degree of restraint, a shred of control. Nothing came through. All I could hear were questions - like whorls of fountains springing up and falling down, standing in a queue, refusing to settle down. No one knocked on the door. No one called. The phone's screen didn't come alive all of a sudden. It lay there, fallen. Silent. Nothing around me could speak. The chill in the air bit me hard. My throat became bulky. I wanted to curl around myself. I brought my arms closer, made tight fists of my hands, till my nails dug into my palms. I stared at the door. I thought of his face. His smile. The look in his eyes that I waited for. That I wanted to have. He stopped looking that way when he announced his decision, and after.

I couldn't get those distant eyes off my mind.

And, I broke down.

# Long Lost

A sky-blue paper bird rested against the mirror of a brown dressing table. She had two tall trapezoidal wings and a downward curved tail. It seemed as if she had just landed by the mirror. The pointed blue beak poked the sturdy glass, and her narrow trunk drooped. But she didn't fall.

She loved origami. From a tender age. We were eight years old. While the rest of us muddied our shirts at football, or at other times, found our ways drawing conical mountains on white paper, rectangular tree trunks and oval lemon-yellow suns, she would snuggle in a corner, her legs folded under her skirt patted down neatly over her knees, her hair-band keeping her curls in check, and start making shapes out of paper. She would make white swans, purple butterflies, green parrots with red beaks, pink frocks, yellow boats with twin seating, and grey cats standing tall with wide faces, triangular ears, and long slender necks. Sometimes she would just crumple a large sheet of paper to make several spikes and pits, and spray-paint it with any colours she found.

It was one of the first things we did together. She didn't mind a sweaty, smelly, muddy, talkative boy sitting next to her, mimicking her finger-moves step-by-step, and yet not quite managing to get the bird right.

"Give. I can do it," she would say.

And I would watch her shape its wings, and my amorphous thoughts. Thoughts I don't recall having for anyone, before her.

I had locked the door of her bedroom, with just the sky-blue bird for company. I began to unbutton my shirt, feeling awkward and confused, and there sat the motionless bird parked against the mirror, staring at me and stirring a lifetime of memories. I went to the door and pressed my ear against it. Outside, she had turned up the volume of the TV.

We were meeting after eight long years. In a foreign country. The United States. Who would have thought? My Mom did!

When I called her from a public phone at London Heathrow, she gushed, "Guess what, Sachin! Nidhi lives in Baltimore!"

"What? Who told you?"

"Her mother called a few hours back. She knew about your travel but didn't know the city."

"And, you told her Baltimore?"

"Of course. What else?"

"Hmm... Nothing."

"Now, message her on Facebook. And, note down her number. Buy a calling card after you arrive there and call her."

"I thought she moved to Canada after her studies."

"Yeah... somehow we all thought that, didn't we?"

"Yeah."

"You know, I feel so much better now. I don't have to worry about how you will manage."

I was relocating in 2010 to the U.S. for a two-year Master's program. This was my first international travel. Mom had been worrying herself to death for weeks over the whole thing. "I'll be fine, Mom."

"No - there is no one else there that we know. That city is unknown. But now you have Nidhi!" The joy dripped from her voice, spilled into the phone and flowed into my ear.

"But I arrive at midnight. I am sure she has to leave for work early in the morning."

"No, No, No! Don't give me excuses. It's just for a day, after all. I don't want you staying at the airport or in a hotel."

"It will be a big hassle for her. We are not in touch anymore. We barely chat."

"Please just stay with her, okay? Tell her not to receive you at the airport, if you wish."

I was silent for a minute. I imagined us... myself at her place, the two of us reclining on parallel couches, watching TV and avoiding eye-contact.

"Sachin?"

"Yeah, I am here."

"Take her address. Call her after you land. She will guide you. All the cabs there have GPS."

"I know!"

"But you don't know—"

"What?"

"That she is your friend."

I closed my eyes and sighed, "Address?"

"Yes." She dictated the address and her number. My fingers dived into my bag and waded through the rustling pages of a notepad, to grab hold of a blank paper.

"Take care. I'm keeping now. I don't want to disturb your Heathrow tour." She kept the phone.

I replaced the receiver on its silver handle. It ruffled a bit, there was no shiver, no jolt. I clutched the handle of my trolley-bag and searched for somewhere to sit. There was an isolated empty chair next to another public phone, a hundred meters away. I rushed over and grabbed the seat. I dropped my sling bag that fell on the floor. I left the slender handle of my trolley-bag, which tremored a little and then stood on its own. I crouched behind a little, to recline on the chair. I stared into space, as far as my eyes could see.

People were queuing at a café. Quiet. Waiting. What were they thinking? That their journeys would end at their destined airports? That their journeys had no surprises in store? That expectation didn't cling to surprises? That having expectation was a strict no-no? I wondered why airports had an air of restlessness, why they were so full of fidgety souls—people wandering, pondering, sleepy, chatty or hungry. Sandwiched between thoughts of travels left behind, people left behind, memories left to wither away, and places that lay ahead, folks waiting in anticipation.

And what about me? Did I harbour feelings for those folks who were etched only in memory? Even today? I was not sure. These questions were strange enough to answer. I had been on a rollercoaster ride. Friendship. Separation. Hurt. Regret. Desolation. Hurt. Normalcy. And humour, at last, or to laugh it off. They were people from the past. Long lost... lost and found.

Nidhi was a year older than me. She answered the SAT and left us, me and our group of friends, to pursue her undergraduate course in the U.S. and took up a job immediately after. I worked for a few years after my Bachelor's in India, before deciding to pursue a Master's abroad. Not the least because she lived there... something me and my mom didn't even know, back then. Her family had literally vanished and kept a good distance from us. No bitterness, but a clear distance. They moved out of our neighbourhood a couple of years before her SAT. So, we had parted even before she left the country.

Maybe I thought too much or connected dots that did not exist... but they moved a month after what had happened... sitting at an airport now, and recalling that episode felt unnecessary. A brief exchange of words, but maybe, it made her uncomfortable. And maybe her parents too. But Nidhi's growing closeness with her school science project mate, Vinay, had angered me. She always got upset with any bad behaviour on my part, but I didn't know what else I could have done.

They had begun to visit each other's homes too often. Their parents got close. And, I had become sillier and more suspicious by the day. We couldn't meet, we couldn't speak. Mobile phones had merely arrived by then. SMS was becoming the norm. Didn't help much. She didn't pick up calls. This project was crucial, even from the future SAT perspective – yes, by then, she had told me that she would be going abroad, which never made it easy for me, when I got to spend some time with her. I gave in to silent spells, sudden temper and strange distressful reactions… and she just kept with it, with all of my moods, till she could. One fine day, I surprised her and Vinay, by going to her home uninvited. Her mom welcomed me in, but I barged into her room. They were jotting down notes, next to a fancy-looking spacecraft. I was a bit embarrassed to see them, because what I thought in my head was different. But she knew:

*"What happened? Why did you—," she fumbled for words.*

*"Why don't you talk to me?"*

*"Sachin, we spoke about it. Remember? And, the reason is in front of you. Can you see it?"*

*"Yes."*

*"Now can we work?"*

*"A project can't change your life."*

*"What?"*

*"And you can't make new friends, just like that."*

*"I can't?"*

*"It's been more than a month. We have stopped speaking. This has never happened between us."*

*"I don't know what you mean. I just want to focus. And, you know why."*

*"Of course you know everything. At least tell me a clear No. But say something."*

*"Please…"*

*"Can we just talk for a minute."*

*"Please go."*

I saw Vinay smirk and look down at his notepad when I made eye-contact. But she fixed her eyes on me, till I stood there for a while, took a deep breath and left without a word.

We did speak after that day. But she always avoided long conversations, even those related to the project. She was having her last days in our neighbourhood. She spent a tiny part of those with me, but more with *all of us,* our group of friends. She wanted to part ways, amicably. She looked for a life ahead, in another country. She solely wanted to see that. I kept my best efforts to stay in touch after she had moved out. But that didn't make a difference.

The years passed. We grew, and grew apart. And, one day, she flew out of India. A few years later, Facebook had arrived. But, somehow she kept a distance with me, although she did call or chat on occasions. To me, her replies were always cordial, terse and formal. Precise. I just never found the friend I had known since I was eight, from those chat windows, the inboxes, the messages, or the machines I got used to talking to. But, over time, I outgrew it. And at one point, I gave up.

A half-hour later, at Heathrow, I went to a row of computers and paid for the internet. I logged into Facebook and messaged her: *"Hi Nidhi, how are you? I am sorry I'm arriving at midnight. I was planning to stay in a hotel but Mom must have told you, or you have an idea, I am assuming. It's just one night. I will leave early tomorrow, for my apartment. The paperwork is done, just that the moving-in date is tomorrow. So, I need to stay somewhere tonight. Sorry, really... for the trouble. I had no idea you were there. You don't have to come to the airport. Okay? I will manage. Please... And, I have your address. Will call you after I arrive. Bye."*

Nine hours later, I found myself at the Baltimore airport. I got a calling card and dialled her number.

"Sachin?" asked the voice from the other side.

"Hi... Nidhi."

"Hey..." she paused for some time.

"Hello...?"

"Have you reached?"

"Yeah. Just took my baggage." I cleared my throat.

"Okay." She paused again. "You have just one?"

"Don't ask. The other one got delayed."

"British Airplanes? They do that - sometimes."

"Do they?"

"Don't worry. I won't let this spoil your first visit."

I thought she smiled. "No, No, I am not panicking." I tried to sound calm.

"You will get your bag tomorrow. Delivered to your apartment, or mine. Which address have you given them?"

"Mine."

"Hmm... Why didn't you want me to come to the airport?"

"Come on!"

"Anyway, it was for the best. I got time to cook rice, *dal*, and *bhindi*. Just so that you don't feel the culture shock!"

"My God. Why did you bother?"

"*Shh…* Now stop talking. Grab a cab and come home."

"It's 12:30. You don't have to wait up for me?"

"Sachin? Please. I can deal with some drowsiness at work tomorrow."

"Okay… I will see you soon."

"Bye." She hung up.

She was right. Getting to meet her was a bigger deal, bigger than the different world I had stepped onto. She had stirred a hornet's nest in my cluttered head, nine hours back. My world had already tumbled upside down. A new country was ignored, at least for some time. I found my way to the exit. What did she think of me? Of this sudden encounter? What would we speak about? Would I be able to hide my nervousness? Why should I be nervous? Unsettling questions. Niggling doubts.

I tried to focus on the here and now, but her memories filled my head. The flashes refused to stop. They were restless, but had meaning. They never took a breather, not even for a minute. Several of them. Some were sharper than others. Dancing in the rain. Dances on stage. Dances at birthday parties. Dancing on the footpath as a *Ganpati* procession passed by on the adjacent street. Sharing secrets. Scaring each other with ghost stories. Walking down that dark, desolated alley when the streetlights didn't work. When she grasped my hand. The alley that led us to her building, where her mother waited: *"So late? What if Sachin wasn't there? How would you have come?"*

Our first fight. When I pushed her, and she fell. No tears. No anger. An emotionless, resolute face. A full ten minutes later, she had punched me back. No warning. I had pretended the blow hurt my arm, though not as much as it actually hurt. Our first *pani-puri*. The first time she learned to cycle. Months later, my first double-seat. And when she fell into a thorny bush? That intricate design of red-brown branches carved on her ankle and her foot. She had hesitated but hadn't stopped me touching it. She didn't wince in pain. They were mean scratches. They pained after an hour. I was paranoid: *"You need an injection right now. My Mom says so!"*

*"I will take it tomorrow morning."*

*"No, let's go. It's not 10 yet. The doctor will be there, I think."*

*"No, I just need to wash it for now. You help me stand. Take me to that tap."*

I did the needful. As I always did. But that's no reason to trust someone. Why had she trusted me? Had she?

And, what should I trust now? My instincts? Should I close my eyes? Stop thinking? Shoo the memories? Stop the flashes? Sitting with a row of desktops at Heathrow, I had stalked her Facebook profile. Caught up on her recent solo treks in the U.S. Smiled at her pictures. It was the first time I had checked her profile, in years. That chapter had ended. Quite clearly, or so I thought.

But, there was no culture shock. *She* was the shock. She was the turn of events. Not the visuals or sounds or people of a changed country.

Getting into a cab, I stared out of the window at the stillness of Baltimore. There was a deathly silence on the freeway. Lovely roads—smooth, spotless, meandering. But hardly a vehicle. It was August. Chilly, though the cab had decent heating. The cabbie was quiet. He asked nothing, relied on the GPS. Kept his head still. After a while, he turned on utterly unfamiliar music. I think it was a short distance. Twenty minutes later, I was at her apartment.

An old, ornate, chocolate-brown building had some ten floors, or so it seemed in the streetlights. I climbed three green-carpeted stairs and stood outside an auto-locked glass door. I called her. She disconnected. I guessed she would be coming down. I stood there, fiddling with my bags. I started twiddling with the airline tags for no reason. I wanted to take them out. I tried to unlock the tight plastic strap that they fixed on the chain. I heard the sound of an elevator, stopping with effort. Yes, it was an old building with those rusted clunky elevators that made you feel like you are being lifted high up. I certainly was...

"Hey." There... I heard her call when the elevator door opened. She turned around to close it and took a few quick steps towards me but slowed down, somewhere in between. A sky-blue t-shirt. Pale blue pyjamas, with small white solid circles and a few random prints of red mushrooms. A beaming smile. Hair left open, straight, over one shoulder. A thin, almost invisible gold chain around her neck. Unusual... she had never cared much for jewellery before. I instinctively glanced at her fingers. Bare. She seemed to have lost weight. Didn't she eat? Didn't she cook for herself? What did she do at home? I knew that she stayed alone. Of course, that didn't mean she was single. I was aware that she had been working for more than a year at an investment bank. She was doing well.

But for my arrival, she should have been in bed now. Her head buried deep in the pillow, this silent city forgotten. She might have been talking in her sleep; she did that sometimes. Or, snoring. No, I will drop that! That was a long time back. The stuff you know from sleepovers and overnight school picnics. When you see your friends' sleeping habits for the first time. I'm not bringing that up!

"Hi, Nidhi." She opened the glass door. I stopped myself from hugging her.

"Hi—" She returned the gesture and held back. "Hi…" The smile dimmed a bit but didn't leave her eyes. Not so soon. "Come in! It's cold. You have just a sweater on."

"Uh… yeah."

"But why?"

"Now don't get started that I need to do this and do that. I know, I am not a local."

She gave a purse-lipped smile, and tried to take the handle of the trolley bag.

"Oh no, I'll take it," I said.

"Give me the other bag then."

I handed over my sling bag.

"You see that?" She pointed to a white tower-like structure in the distance.

"What's that?"

"The Washington Monument. The older one. The one in DC came later."

"Nice. Right outside your apartment, huh?"

"Yeah," she gleamed with pride.

"You love that, don't you?" I thought I could tease.

"Yes! Now, let's eat. Your food is ready."

"Hope you didn't wait… Did you eat something?"

"Nah, I had something in the evening, don't worry."

It was deliberate. Switching our thoughts to food. Driving all the way upstairs, any helpless bits that were left unspoken. But what else could she do? It's awkward when two ex-buddies, completely out of touch, meet after almost a decade. Thorny. Problematic. Greetings are incomplete. Formality is pervasive. Words are measured. In the elevator, my bags huddled against each other at the centre, in the space between us. A pathetic barricade. She took one wall. I took the other. She peered at my bags, at the airline tags hanging on them, at their design and their details. Why? Who knows, ask her! I looked at the door. I waited for the third floor, as the elevator climbed up lazily. I waited most artificially, most falsely and most stupidly.

She opened the door to her apartment. I parked my bags by the side.

"No, take them to that room. That's your room."

"Oh. Okay." I did as I was told. Surely there were two rooms. I wasn't so stupid.

She made herself busy in the kitchen. Checked the *bhindi.* Set out the plates. Poured water in two glasses. None of which was an emergency, but she got occupied and wordless. I went into my room, kept my bags. I opened the suitcase to pull out some clothes. I gently pushed the door to check if it would close on its own. It didn't shut completely. I pushed it further. It clicked shut. I searched for a proper track-pant and a t-shirt. I didn't feel comfortable wearing shorts, though that's what I usually wore at home. How silly! We have been there, done that. As buddies swimming together, playing in water-parks, as teenagers dancing in the rain. As friends having multiple sleepovers at each other's homes. Alright, it might have been years ago. Ages ago. But what was *this*? What was stopping me? What was I doing?

"Sachin?" I heard her call from the kitchen.

"Yeah?"

"You want to shower? There's an attached bathroom."

"Oh...uh...okay. I will be out in some time."

"Okay."

"But the food will get cold, right?"

"Don't worry about that." I heard her footsteps receding.

That's when I caught sight of the blue paper-bird. Parked by the mirror. And that's when I went into a spell. Pulling out of it, I unbuttoned my shirt and went into the shower. I turned it on and let the hot water hit my face, the currents stream down my skin, carry the fatigue down the drain, and just maybe, crush a few incessant thoughts in my head.

I stepped out in a black track-pant and a white t-shirt. Upon seeing me, she lowered the TV volume. No sooner had I stepped out than she blurted:

"Are you calmer now?"

"Huh?"

"You seemed a bit uneasy."

"Me?"

"Downstairs."

"No. I am fine. Really."

The table was set. She started serving the food.

"Oh, you sit down too. I will help myself."

"No, relax. I don't have guests here very often. Let me do it." She chuckled.

"Yeah right! I am a guest."

"You are behaving like one."

"Huh?"

"You have quietened over the years."

"Huh?"

"Huh?" she mimicked me. "What's wrong with you? Or, maybe I shouldn't ask. You are tired."

"Yeah, a little. But better now. After the shower. *Umm*, this tastes so good!" I munched on the *bhindi*.

"Really?"

"It's yummy. I am suddenly hungry now."

"Thank you." She smiled, with a faint blush.

"So…?" I swallowed the rice. "Why did you say that?"

"What?"

"That you don't have guests."

"I stay alone." She full-stopped it, right there. Poured some more *dal* over the rice on her plate. Positioned her plate. Avoided looking at me. I waited.

"And?" I asked her.

"And I like, that." The words popped out with effort. "I don't want roommates. And, Baltimore has few visitors, anyway. I love my work. Immensely."

She gave that emphatic *'Imm'*, more than was necessary. The spoon in her hand gently slipped into her mouth. She gazed in front of her, fixed herself on the music system in the lower rack below the TV. She held a long empty stare. Unnerving.

"Can I ask you something?" A million voices in my head yelled at me out of nowhere. *'Stupid' 'Fool' 'Crazy'*

*'Silly'* and a hundred other mocking words. They knew my intent. They pulled me to stop.

"No, you may not!" She grinned.

I closed my eyes, irked. "Look this may sound silly."

"I know. I can see that."

"*Shh* - Aren't you dating anyone?"

Now, she looked me in the eye.

"I mean—", I pretended to chew. "You are settled. You have stayed here for a few years now. I mean, serious dating?" I floundered, cringing at my question, or its idiotic framing, or its embarrassing timing, or the choice of words, or the desperation, or whatever, I don't know what! This is what happens when you meet your ex-'flame' after many many years – if I could even think like that. A flame warped by time.

But she giggled. She bought time by pouring some more water into her glass. After she had taken a few sips, she said, "No. I am not dating anyone. Seriously or frivolously. I hang out with people. Yes. Few office colleagues. Few Indians I have got to know. You can say, friends. No dates, yet."

"Why?"

"Don't know."

"Tell me."

"Really. I mean, there are interesting peoplc. I won't say I didn't find anybody. But I don't know. I am not sure what they are looking for, or if they want to date."

"They asked you out?"

"*They*?" She giggled again.

"I mean, this one, that one, whoever!"

"Yeah. A few of them. I agreed. But they weren't dates, eventually. Just conversations. Over coffee."

"Hmm... you can call that a date."

"Not me, I can't."

"Why?"

"Come on, we are having a conversation right now. After years, and, we know this isn't a date." She smiled through the corners of her lips and resumed chewing.

I didn't like the sound of that. What was the need to bring me into the topic? Why the tease? She increased the volume of the TV and pretended to catch up on some earth-shattering headline story. As if that was urgent. Had I annoyed her? I was a fool. Confused. Why didn't I listen to the voices in my head? I had just recovered from the travel fatigue and the anticipation of meeting her. I first needed to trust my instincts. Even if I was, then, a bloody shy, hesitant, obnoxiously inhibited loser!

"You look different," she said, puncturing into my self-recrimination.

"In what way?"

"You have gained weight."

"Oh, really?" I reflexively straightened and tucked in a bit of my tummy.

"But that's good. You were so lanky, back then. All bones."

"You remember?"

"Of course. Everything."

"I remembered too. After looking at that bird. The sky-blue bird on your dresser."

She turned away from the TV, towards me, and looked straight into my tired, jet-lagged eyes. The slow, inhibited smile widened into a delightful grin.

"You saw it?" Her eyes glinted.

"Yeah. And, I remembered our paper folding."

"And how you used to mess it up?"

"And how you always teased me about it."

"And how you cried that you would never get it right."

"And how you teased that I wouldn't ever get it right."

"And how you tried again and again, sobbing and sulking?"

"And how you helped me fix it."

"Yeah!" She laughed.

"Cruel."

"I am. I still don't think you can make even a half-decent boat!"

"Shut up."

But she had the last word. She laughed a bit more, demolishing some of the distances between us.

No, it was not the geography that had come in between. Nor the time zones. Nor the busy lives. Nor the divergent careers. Nor the priorities. Nor the formality. It was the silence of this barren living room. The staring uncaring closets of the kitchen. The staring lamps. The empty chairs across the dining table. The rough carpet. The darkness outside the window. The lack of noise on the street. The screechy news on TV. The fact that its volume had to be lowered for a conversation to take place. That our voices were structured and led by the rule-book. The fact that television could disturb us. The two glasses of water that were placed a foot away. The feet below the table that didn't dare to touch each other. The secretive looks that didn't dare to meet. We didn't need a different country to create distance. We made distance by not pulling our chairs close together. The distance, was that I couldn't tease her like before. Couldn't tap her on her head. Couldn't poke her. Crack silly jokes. Argue. Grab her spoon, if she bugged me. The distance was that I could not hug her, or even hold her. That I was inept. Inept to make her feel, for a moment at least, that she was having a date, a real date. A date with a childhood friend. At midnight. In the middle of a repressed, muted living room. In a sleeping city with no one to intrude. Yes, she was with someone who could be trusted. Who could make her laugh. Who carried fond memories, and, a touch of origami.

"Where do you keep disappearing?" Once again, she intruded into my thoughts.

"As in?"

"What do you keep falling into, every now and then? Thoughts? Or spells?"

"I didn't fall. You caught me."

"I keep an eye out."

"Thank you."

"But where were you?"

"I wander."

"Wander?"

"Yeah." I breathed in.

"But you didn't, back then. You used to talk. Non-stop. Chitter-Chatter."

"I do talk even now. Sometimes."

"And why not often?"

"There are reasons. I think it's a waste of time to chitter-chatter for the sake of it."

"That's your view. And hard to believe, considering what you were." She shot me a quick, curious glance.

"That was different. A different time. Different people."

She had her means to deflect my remarks like these. She could play with the spoon and the rice slipping in and out of it. She could reposition her plate. She could tuck away an errant lock of hair behind her ear. Or, she could divert the conversation to an earlier remark, which she did.

"You are not wandering," she said.

"How do you know?"

"You have come for your Master's. At a very good university. You have goals, clearly."

"That could just add to it."

"Oh, so you are anxious about how it will go?"

"I am anxious." I paused. "I am anxious for the same reasons as you are."

"Who says I am anxious?"

"You."

"Huh?"

"That there are no guests here." I almost heard myself blurting that out.

"So?"

"That wasn't just a statement."

She kept the spoon down on her plate. It rattled a bit.

She touched it, straightened it a little. "You are getting it all wrong. I don't feel the need for anyone here. I told you."

"Yeah, you told me."

"I don't want to share my apartment."

"Okay. I will take it back. Let's not argue."

"Sachin, I love this space."

"You do know that it's not about this space, don't you?"

"Sachin!"

"You want me to leave?"

"What?"

"To my apartment, right now?"

"Don't talk rubbish," she spoke a bit loudly.

I should have stopped it there, but my words raced against me.

"You want me to go tomorrow?"

"You *have* to go tomorrow," she said.

"But do you *want* me to? I am not obliged to."

"I have to go to work. I am obliged to," she said.

"Are you?"

"What's happening to you?"

"You wanted me to chitter-chatter. I am doing that."

"No. You are doing something else." She fidgeted.

"What am I doing?"

"Have you really quietened?"

"I have. If that's what you want to hear."

"It's not about me," she said.

"I see pain. And it tears me apart."

"There is no pain. And you are not healing anything." She raised her voice.

"Like you know everything?"

"Whose pain, Sachin?"

That shut me up for a moment. But I went on. "Then, why even share? With me? Why blurt it out? Why indicate that…?"

"Indicate what?"

"That there is no one."

"I am not clarifying. Again."

"You want me to clarify? Using the most appropriate words?"

"Stop it. Eat. Please."

"Am I being a guest now?"

"Sachin… we are meeting after so long," she said, her voice muffling under its weight.

"Then we better talk, right?"

There was no answer. She turned the volume of the television higher. I felt like snatching the remote and hurling it at the black windows. Smashing them. They were sturdy enough. They wouldn't really break. Like I would muster the energy to snatch the remote for real! My thoughts were simply waves of words and symbols racing in my head. They were easy to conjure, but they added up to nothing. I could take no action. Ask no question that was specific. Because I couldn't take 'No' for an answer, but could only get restless about it. It's not that I had longed for her every day for eight years. But I covered the emptiness. Bridged the gaps. With studying. Work. Knowledge. Friends. Social circles. Dates.

Fun. More importantly, with routines. It looked like she too had done some of that. And yet, now, that I was with her, I could barely speak. Except that I said things to unsettle her, and drive her back behind the television. Gave in to my impulses. My futile impulses.

We did resume our conversation. We changed topics. We calmed down, or acted like we had. We diverted our minds to the rice and the *dal* and the garlic *chutney* and the pickle. We talked about our lives or how had they been, we talked about our jobs, our bosses, our decisions and our families. We did talk a little more about our childhood. Our friends. Where had they vanished? Those who married too early. Those who took to alcohol. Those who remained cold and distant. Those who changed, or those who still called in the wee hours of the night, crying like babies. Those who sent long, effusive chat messages. But we didn't talk about, us. We finished dinner. We cleaned the plates and the spoons. We chatted for a bit. And we retreated to our respective rooms to sleep. Perhaps with open eyes. At least I did.

On my bed, I tossed and turned. I couldn't sleep for a good length of time. I didn't want to count sheep. I made up images, instead. I visualized two people. Couldn't stop myself. Nidhi and Sachin. My mind conjured up a conversation between these two. Not in a dream. Nor in real life. Somewhere in between. Stuck in limbo.

We are dining. I have set a table. Like she had, an hour ago. Our chairs are close together. The TV has been turned off, for good. We are giggling at sweet silly nothings. She's feeding me a spoonful of rice. We are looking into each other's eyes, absolutely not missing a single glance. We are chatting. Talking about things that matter. Laughing. Loving.

"Should we live here, in this country I mean?" I ask her.

"Will I work with this company forever? I don't think so."

"You will get another job."

"Hmm…" She searches for an answer.

"I will complete my Master's. Then, a Ph.D. That's seven years. I could get used to this place, its people, its ways. Then, I won't feel like moving elsewhere." I go in explaining mode.

"So, what would you feel? Staying with me?"

"You are not a bad roomie," I tell her.

"Really? It's been ages we had a sleepover. We were kids back then."

"But you are pretty," I smirk, "How often would I get a pretty roomie?"

"Then, let's stay here," she says.

"And marry?"

"Yeah. Why? Do you want to live in?"

"Not sure. You?"

"I don't think so," she says.

"Oh, Okay. Hmm. Okay!"

"Let's get married. Even though the thought makes me ultra-anxious," she says the last part softly, but she still looks at me.

"But you know me. Your muddy buddy from childhood. One who now thinks, and asks questions. Lots of them. The subdued chatter-box. That should make you less anxious."

"Yeah right!"

I nodded at that, shook my head vigorously. And, the images vanished. The conversation ended. The scene I made in my mind blew away like a broken eyelash from the top of a fist. But, at least the talk ended on that note. An ending that I decided. But could I decide anything outside my head, outside this room, outside my comfort zone? Did I have any shred of a choice, with her? It was 2 a.m. I deliberated on my choices for the next fifteen minutes. I had to do it. I had to do something.

I got up. I opened the door. I walked towards her room. I took a deep breath. I knocked on her door. I kept telling myself: Nidhi, please don't take me wrong! Don't judge! Don't freak out! Talk to me! At least, open the door!

"Yeah?" came the muffled voice from inside.

"You are not sleeping, are you?"

There was no answer.

"Nidhi?"

No answer.

"Nidhi, I am sorry, were you sleeping?"

No answer.

"Nidhi?"

She opened the door. No, her eyes didn't look sleepy. No, she didn't look startled, annoyed or disturbed. No, she wasn't asleep. Just a bit surprised.

"I can't sleep. I want to talk," I said.

She sighed and looked away, inspecting the carpet.

"No, you don't say anything. You don't have to. Let's have coffee. I will make it. Okay? Tell me where it's kept. That first closet there? That one?"

"You are jet-lagged." She smiled.

"Fine. Dismiss me. Think what you want. But let me talk to you. Anything that comes to my head. Just hear me out. Bear with me. Have your coffee. Yawn when you want. Giggle when you want. Mock me. Since you are not sleepy, you won't doze off. Since I am jet-lagged, I won't doze off. So, just hear me out? Okay? Where should we sit? At the table?"

Again, the smile didn't quite leave her eyes. She bit her lip, to gather any words she had to utter, or so I thought. "You won't ask me difficult questions?" she asked.

"No."

"You won't talk about the future?"

"No."

"You won't talk about moving to your apartment in the middle of the night?"

"No"

"You will be okay?"

"I think so."

"You will be a friend?"

"Of course."

"As you were back then?"

"More or less."

"Are you the same person?"

"I think so."

"You will make birds and boats?"

"Yes."

"Actual birds and boats?"

"No."

"Better birds and boats?"

"I will try."

"Am I asking for too much?"

"No."

"Aiming for the stars?"

"Hmm? No."

"Is this, whatever is going on—"

"Shh!" I stopped her.

"Okay," she stopped.

"Shall we?"

"Yeah. Go on. Make coffee."

www.ingramcontent.com/pod-product-compliance
Ingram Content Group UK Ltd.
Pitfield, Milton Keynes, MK11 3LW, UK
UKHW022235230426
12048UKWH0018BA/1272